THE BLACK STALLION SERIES
by Steven Farley

The Black Stallion's Shadow
The Black Stallion's Steeplechaser

THE BLACK STALLION SERIES
by Walter Farley

The Black Stallion
The Black Stallion Returns
Son of the Black Stallion
The Island Stallion
The Black Stallion's Blood Bay Colt
The Black Stallion's Courage
The Black Stallion Mystery
The Black Stallion and Flame
Man o'War
The Black Stallion's Ghost
The Black Stallion and the Girl
The Black Stallion Legend
The Young Black Stallion (with Steven Farley)

STEVEN FARLEY

Random House ⌂ New York

http://www.randomhouse.com/

Library of Congress Cataloging-in-Publication Data:
Farley, Steven. The black stallion's steeplechaser / by Steven Farley.
p. cm. — (The Black stallion series)
SUMMARY: Alec Ramsay tries to hold on to his love of racing
and his steeplechaser Black Storm when both are threatened under
different circumstances.
ISBN: 0-679-88200-6 (trade) — 0-679-98200-0 (lib. bdg.)
1. Horses—Juvenile fiction. [1. Horses—Fiction.] I. Title.
II. Series: Farley, Walter. Black Stallion series.
PZ10.3.F215B1 1997 [Fic]—dc20 96-31035

Printed in the United States of America 10 9 8 7 6 5 4 3 2 1

For Mom, Dad, Pam, Alice, and Tim

Contents

CHAPTER ONE

A Brand-New Challenge

It was a great day for a horse race, a warm afternoon in early June. Alec Ramsay felt excited and more than a little anxious as he filed toward the paddock at New York's Belmont Park Racetrack with the other jockeys. Post time for the Ganymede Steeplechase was fast approaching, and this race was going to be especially important.

Alec, eighteen years old with flashing blue eyes and an easy smile, was a top-ranked jockey at tracks throughout the country, thanks to a fantastic stallion named the Black. Here in New York, he was something of a hometown hero.

Clinton Smith, a regular rider at Belmont, swaggered up beside Alec and tapped the younger jockey on the shoulder with the butt of his riding whip.

"Well, if it isn't the Boy Wonder himself," Smith said with a friendly wink. He was a short blond-haired man with long sideburns. "What are you doing in this race, kid? I didn't know you rode in 'chases."

Alec shrugged. He liked Smith well enough, but he wasn't overly eager to advertise the fact that this was his very first steeplechase.

"Live and learn, Clint," said Alec.

"Who you riding today, anyway?"

"Black Storm," Alec answered curtly.

"Another one of the Black's colts, huh?"

Alec nodded. "Yeah. This one is really special." He tilted back his riding helmet and pushed away a few strands of red hair that were falling in front of his eyes.

Smith adjusted the strap on his riding helmet. "Almost won a 'chase upstate last month." He nodded toward a jockey in green silks who was also making his way across the lawn to the paddock. "Know who that is? Tom Hall. He and that old war-horse of his are gonna be the ones we have to look out for."

Alec glanced at the jockey in the green silks. From studying the racing form, he knew that Tom Hall was a veteran rider who specialized in steeple-chases. He also knew that Hall's mount, a six-year-

2

old chestnut gelding named Chazz, was the favorite to win the Ganymede Steeplechase today.

Tom Hall saw Alec eyeing him. He walked over and stretched out his hand. "It's a pleasure meeting you, sir. The name's Hall. Tom Hall. From Virginia, sir."

Alec shook the jockey's hand. Hall was fairly heavyset for a jockey. With his big smile and dark, handsome features, he looked more like a professional tennis player or golfer. "Nice to meet you, too," Alec said.

"My agent tells me this is going to be your first 'chase. Welcome aboard."

Smith's brows lifted at this bit of information. Alec felt his face flush.

"Don't worry, son," Hall said, giving Alec a friendly salute. "Anyone who can ride a horse like the Black shouldn't have too much trouble with a few hurdles."

Hall headed off to find his horse. Smith turned to Alec again, a slight smirk creasing his lips. "Well, well, well," he said. "What do you know? So this is Boy Wonder's first 'chase."

"Quit calling me that, will you?" Alec snapped.

Smith's little smile turned into a good-natured laugh. "I'm just kidding around, kid. Don't get mad. I'm jealous, that's all."

Alec sighed. "Sure, Clint."

Smith put his arm around Alec's shoulder. "Come on now, buddy. I've only been in a handful of 'chases myself. I'm really a flat-track rider, just like you. And if that colt of yours can run anything like his daddy, you should make out just fine today. *If you can keep your boots in your stirrups, that is.*"

Alec shrugged Clint's arm off his shoulder. "Who do you think you're talking to, Clint? It isn't like this is my first time around a turf course, you know."

"It'll still be your first time over hurdles under real racing conditions, right? That colt of yours ever been over this course?"

"Just in a light workout yesterday," Alec admitted.

"He ever even been ridden in a 'chase before?"

Alec shook his head. "Anything else you'd like to know, Clint?" he said testily. "Like what I had for breakfast, maybe?"

Smith whistled and held up his hands. "Hey, I'm no one to talk," he said. "Matter of fact, I got thrown in my last 'chase."

"Really?" Alec asked. "I thought you almost won."

Smith shrugged. "Wasn't the first time I've been tossed in a 'chase. Doubt if it'll be the last, either."

He pointed to a small dent in his helmet. "See that?"

Alec chuckled at the other jockey's gung-ho bravado. "Why do you keep riding in steeplechases then, if it's so dangerous?"

"Just crazy, I guess. It's a kick. All that speeding up, slowing down, jumping, and landing. Wait till you try it in traffic."

Alec remembered the thrilling stories old Max Dwyer had told him about his days riding steeplechases back in Ireland. If it hadn't been for Max visiting Hopeful Farm last winter, Alec probably wouldn't even be here at Belmont today. Max was the one who had suggested Storm as a potential steeplechaser in the first place. After the Irishman had returned home, Alec had become dead serious about wanting to give steeplechasing a "go," as Max would say.

Smith smiled at Alec. "So what are you planning to do with all your prize money after you win this thing?" he asked as the two of them continued on their way to the paddock.

"That's a joke," Alec said. "Storm and I'll be lucky to—"

Just then, there was a loud commotion up ahead. A horse was shrilling loudly. Alec recognized the source of the racket: Black Storm. Another shrill blast from the rambunctious colt cut through the air, followed by a booming "Whoa!" from veteran trainer Henry Dailey.

"Never a dull moment," Alec quipped to Clint. "See you at the gate." He turned and jogged through the crowded paddock to join Henry and Black Storm outside the saddling shed.

"Whoa!" Henry ordered Storm again.

The colt half-reared up onto his hind legs. Trainers and grooms on either side quickly moved their horses away from the fractious colt.

Even if he hadn't been causing so much trouble, Black Storm would still have stood out from the other horses in the paddock. The colt was tall and powerful in build, his lines smooth and bold, his coat jet-black except for the crooked silver blaze on his forehead. His head was large yet well proportioned to his overall size, with a crest that would one day develop the majestic dimension of his sire, the Black.

Storm snorted at Henry and shook his head. *What an animal,* Alec thought admiringly. The colt was as beautiful and smart as he was bad mannered, always intent on getting his own way. Storm continued to fuss and fume, seeming to know just how far he could push Henry before the trainer reached his boiling point.

From deep within the colt's throat came a rumbling noise that sounded like a growl. The colt started to rear up again. Henry responded by snapping the colt's lead line. Storm tugged back. The old trainer's square jaw stuck out like a bulldog's, and deep furrows wrinkled his forehead.

Alec stepped up and took the lead from Henry. "Here, let me try."

The trainer handed the lead line to Alec. "Be my guest."

"Easy, Storm," Alec said soothingly. "Easy now. What do you want to get everyone all worked up for?"

Storm shook his head again but stopped his growling. He eyed Alec and Henry suspiciously. When Alec called to him again, the colt twisted his ears in annoyance and pawed the ground with his hoofs.

Henry shook his head angrily. "If he keeps trying to get away with this nonsense, I'll pull him out of the race. I swear I'll do it."

"He's just bluffing, Henry," Alec said. "You know that."

A bay colt standing on the other side of the paddock called to Storm. Storm immediately pricked up his ears and gave a muffled neigh in reply. After a few moments, the rowdy horse began to settle down. The other trainers and jockeys in the paddock slowly turned their attention back to their own horses.

Storm stood still, staring at Alec as if nothing had happened. Suddenly, he looked as innocent as a lamb.

"Sometimes you can be a real pain, Storm—you know that?" Alec said with a sigh. He wished he could pinpoint just what it was about Storm that told him, *This is a racehorse.* Intuition, maybe. But a mere gut feeling wasn't enough to convince Henry that Storm was worth all the time and energy Alec wanted to put into him. Henry didn't buy intuition.

The old trainer tugged at Storm's belly band. "You're crazy, kid," he grumbled to Alec. "I'm telling you, you're just plain crazy."

"I heard you the first time, Henry."

"This whole steeplechasing idea is nuts. Even if you win, what's the purse? A few lousy bucks? Where's the payoff?"

"We've been over this a hundred times, Henry. Can't we just agree to disagree this once? Besides, I'm the one who's doing the riding. Hey, it might even be fun."

"*Fun?*" Henry spat out the word with a sour face. He stepped closer and Alec saw a hint of concern appear in the trainer's eyes. "What if you get hurt?" Henry demanded. "Our season is just beginning, and you have plenty of other races to ride. Why you're so obsessed to start 'chasing is beyond me, especially on a horse like Storm. The colt is a lunatic, I tell you."

Alec sighed. "We're not going to be jumping fences, Henry. Just low brush hurdles."

"It's all that Irishman's fault," Henry went on bitterly. "If Max hadn't filled your head with all those ridiculous stories…"

Just then, the call for "Riders up!" crackled over the loudspeaker system.

Henry checked Storm's saddle again, then turned to Alec. "Mount up, Alec. Let's get this freak show over with."

Alec took the reins in one hand and with the other rubbed Storm on the neck. The colt seemed relaxed. Alec swung himself lightly into the saddle. Henry scowled and shook his head.

Alec grinned. "If we can make it through the post parade without Storm getting spooked, we might be okay."

"Humph." Henry gave Alec and Storm a hard look as they left the paddock and made their way toward the track. "Just don't break anything," Henry called after them. "You hear me, Alec?"

Alec nodded without turning around. "I hear you, Henry," he called back. Then he followed the rest of the horses out onto the track.

Alec adjusted his helmet. The tension that had

been building between him and Henry over Storm during the past few weeks was coming to a head, Alec knew. The simple fact was that Henry had already made up his mind about Storm and steeple-chasing. As far as the trainer was concerned, the whole thing was a waste of time.

But Black Storm seemed eager to run. He tossed his head defiantly as they trotted off with the other horses and riders. Alec shifted his weight in the saddle and spoke softly to the colt. "Easy, fella. Don't start showing off again. That's it. That's a boy."

He gently rubbed Storm's neck and mentally ran through the jumps in the racecourse ahead. *This is it,* Alec thought. Now everything was up to him and Storm.

CHAPTER TWO

Close Call

The horses passed the grandstand and trotted on toward the backstretch and the starting line. Alec rode as gently as possible, standing in his stirrups as he might have done pulling up at the end of a race. He tracked a quiet horse ahead of him, hoping it would have a calming influence on Storm.

Sweat was already lathering on Storm's flanks, yet they hadn't even reached the post—not a very encouraging sign. Suddenly, Storm broke into an unruly canter. Alec shortened his rein and moved the bit slightly in Storm's mouth to keep the colt from taking a firm hold of it.

Storm slowed to a walk as Tom Hall and Chazz pulled up on the left. The burly chestnut-colored horse held his head to one side, looking at Storm critically, as if sizing him up for the battle ahead. Hall's face was tight and serious, his expression determined. Alec guessed that the Virginian was feeling the pressure of being the favorite.

A moment later, Clint Smith appeared on Alec's right, riding a big bay gelding. "Good luck, rookie. Let's get her done," he said, touching the brim of his helmet with his whip.

"Tallyho!" Alec called after him.

When they reached the start, Alec saw that, unlike a regular race, there was no gate in which to load the horses. Instead, a white elastic ribbon stretched across the track in front of them. The horses took their positions at the line.

Nine hurdles were positioned evenly around the one-and-one-quarter-mile inner-turf course. All of the hurdles were thick green brush fences. Only four feet high, the brush was fitted into long, low wooden frames and secured to the ground. The forgiving nature of the brush, Alec knew, meant that hitting a hedge would be far less hazardous than if the steeplechasers had been jumping over fences. Horses' legs often became bruised from hitting the top bar of a steeplechase fence and tumbling over.

So far so good, Alec thought. At least he'd gotten through the post parade without the hotheaded Storm dumping him. He mentally went over his pre-race checklist: tack adjusted correctly, stirrup the right length, leathers flat against his shinbones, reins knotted. Reaching down to test the girth strap, he made sure it was tight—but not too tight—and pulled it up a notch.

Alec noted the condition of the turf. It was clean and spongy, ideal for both running and jumping. Satisfied, he took a few deep breaths to settle his nerves.

The starter, wearing an official Belmont Park cap, stood off to the side of the field of horses, holding up her right hand. Alec watched the woman from the corner of his eye, looking for a telltale sign that might help him get a jump on the others. Suddenly, the starter's mouth moved slightly, no more than a twitch. Alec squeezed his legs. Down went the starter's hand, and the ribbon snapped away. The horses surged forward in a ragged line.

Alec and Storm's tiny advantage at the start helped the colt break perfectly from his midfield position. Alec sat still and confident, his posture no different from a race with no jumps at all. Almost instantly, Storm began loping along with a smooth, springy stride, already in top gear, the tips of his black ears almost touching.

Seconds later, Storm accelerated into a mad gallop, flattening out to the turf beneath his hoofs, his mane streaming. "Easy, Storm, easy," Alec called to his mount.

Horses moved up on either side of them, and the field began to spread out. Storm was among the four leaders as they approached the first fence. Alec couldn't be sure who the other three horses were. All of his attention remained riveted on the V-shaped window between Storm's ears.

The first brush fence rushed toward them, and the roar of the crowd swelled. Ahead, Alec saw two horses approaching the hedge at flat-track racing speed. As the obstacle rose up in their path, one horse slowed. The other swerved. Alec tried to place Storm between them so that the colt could see what he was doing and stay out of trouble.

Alec felt Storm hesitate slightly as he measured his takeoff. Alec kicked the horse into it with his heels, precisely the signal Storm had been waiting for. The colt soared off the ground.

There was a swishing sound as several horses in unison brushed the top of the fence. It was followed by a silence as they hung in the air for a moment, at the arcs of their jumps. Then came the critical split second as their hoofs touched the ground. Storm's jump took him into second place, just behind and to the right of the leader.

Alec heard shouts, jolts, and bumps behind him

as other horses and riders landed. Then, apart from the horse on his left, the other runners suddenly ceased to exist for Alec. The drumming of hoofs was drowned out by the thuds that came from his own horse. Alec felt exhilarated to have the first hurdle behind them, but ahead lay a long, weary struggle over eight more.

Black Storm jumped the second hedge as neatly as he had the first—smoothly, if a bit too high, and carefully. Chazz was out front. Alec decided to let Storm settle down to the rear of the chestnut favorite. That way, the colt could see how the track should be handled.

As they swept around the turn and headed into the third jump, three horses drew alongside Black Storm. All together, they met the obstacle and sprang into the air. One came down badly and fell. He slid sideways, caught the horse next to him, and knocked him over. Alec winced, but he couldn't concern himself now about the fallen horses and riders. He had to stay focused on what lay ahead.

For another jump and the next turn, Chazz and Storm held their positions. Pulling into the stretch, Chazz moved a bit wide, allowing Storm to move up on the inside. Tom Hall rode confidently, rocking gently to Chazz's long, easy strides. Black Storm drew up beside the chestnut and took a small lead approaching the next hedge. *Storm seems to have the knack of jumping now,* Alec thought. His confidence in Storm redoubled. The bad-mannered son of the Black was showing them all up today.

Alec glanced over his shoulder to see Clint Smith working frantically to get more speed from his big, rangy mount. Soon Smith was closing the gap between himself and the two front runners. Hall allowed Alec and Black Storm to move into the lead by half a length. The Virginian sat still in his seat, seemingly unconcerned. Smith wasn't helping his horse at all. He skated around in his saddle, wriggling and bouncing.

Hall threw his mount into top gear approaching the jump, landing a good length in front of Storm. The colt dug in and moved after the chestnut leader again. Both horses were still full of run.

Now big, bold Chazz flung everything that he had into the race. The arcs of his jumps were wide and low—dangerously low.

Side by side, Storm and Chazz bore down on the next hedge. Hall's eyes burned with determination as he glanced over at Alec. "Not this time, Ramsay!" he called out. But the momentary lapse in concentration on his own horse took its toll. The chestnut suddenly faltered, and Hall failed to steady him soon enough.

He met the hurdle out of stride and hit the brush hard.

As Chazz recovered, Alec tried to sweep past him, but this time Storm's usual accuracy deserted him and the colt staggered slightly on landing. Storm didn't fall, but Alec lost his balance. His boots left their stirrups, and he was immediately launched out of his saddle. As he flew through the air, he could hear Hall shout, "See ya!" The journey was over.

Alec quickly pulled his legs under him, a second before the ground came slamming into him. He tucked into a ball as best he could, cartwheeling under the inside rail and off the track.

In real time, the whole sequence of events had probably taken just a few seconds. But to Alec, in the slow motion of crisis time, it seemed to last forever. Finally the jangled sky stopped spinning above him.

Alec lay motionless on his back for a moment, then crawled to his feet. He felt winded but not seriously injured anywhere. The only thing that really hurt was his pride. He knew the spill was his fault. He'd blown the race for Storm. "How could I be so stupid?" he grumbled aloud. He felt like kicking himself.

Alec looked over to see three track assistants chasing Storm and another loose mount across the turf toward the infield. The rest of the horses and riders raced on toward the finish line, with Chazz and Tom Hall leading the way to victory.

Dusting himself off, Alec began to hobble toward the underpass to the jockey's room. What was it he had been going to prove to Henry? He was going to show them all. Sure.

He clenched his fists, and the numbness in his left wrist became a painful throb. It probably wasn't broken, but he knew he'd better have the track doctor check it out.

Alec winced. *Welcome to the wide world of steeplechasing, Boy Wonder,* he told himself.

CHAPTER THREE

Trouble on the Road

Two hours later, Alec and Henry began loading Storm into the Hopeful Farm van. Alec's wrist still felt stiff, and a stinging pain flared up his arm whenever he moved it. The track doctor had told Alec his injuries might keep him out of the saddle for a few days. *Not if I can help it,* Alec thought.

The guard standing by the entrance gate waved them on as Alec eased the horse van out onto the two-lane road that connected Belmont with the Long Island Expressway. Henry wasn't very happy, Alec could tell, but the old trainer didn't say anything. He just sat there with his fedora pulled low over his forehead and his long, wrinkled face drooping solemnly. Alec decided he'd better break the silence on the subject of the race.

"The colt ran like a champ, Henry. I'm telling you, what happened was all my fault."

Henry cut Alec off with a grunt. "Bad luck, kid. Don't let it bug you." The trainer kept his eyes fixed out the side window.

Alec wondered what Henry was really thinking. "Next time it'll be different," he said.

"Maybe. If there *is* a next time. We're all dealing in perishable goods, Alec. Yourself included. Why you want to make the odds worse by jumping hurdles is beyond me."

Alec squeezed the steering wheel in frustration, and his wrist immediately began to throb. Well, he told himself, Storm had given him a decent shot and he'd pretty much blown it. Maybe Henry was right about this whole steeplechasing thing. But he was dead wrong about Storm.

Alec turned onto the parkway that ran along the tip of Manhattan. Towering steel skyscrapers reflected silver and gold in the light from the setting sun as an oil tanker plowed its way through the outgoing tide. Gulls flew over the docks on the Brooklyn waterfront.

"Kinda pretty, huh?" said Alec, nodding toward the jagged skyline. It was always dramatic, no matter how many times he saw it.

Henry snorted and shook his head. "Pollution," he said.

Alec raised his eyebrows. "What?"

"Streets filled with garbage. Air's polluted. Water. Even us, our brains are polluted. Too much TV. Too much noise."

"Come on, Henry," Alec said, chuckling. "It's not that bad."

Henry turned his gaze toward Alec. "You been back to the old neighborhood recently? In Flushing, where we met?"

Alec shrugged. "Not for a couple of years. How about you?"

Henry nodded. "Visited some friends there last month. That place has really changed. More people, more houses. I don't think you could even keep a horse there nowadays."

"It was crowded enough when we lived there," Alec said.

"You should see it now."

Alec smiled, remembering some of the secret places where he used to ride with the Black. "Living upstate is great, but I sort of miss the old hometown sometimes."

Henry shook his head and stared across the river. A frown turned his lips into an upside-down U.

Alec gathered that the conversation was now over and concentrated on the traffic ahead of him.

As they followed the outline of Manhattan, Alec began to notice a grinding sound every time he switched gears. The sound quickly grew worse.

"What's the matter with you, Alec?" Henry asked. "You're going to strip the gears! Use the clutch, for heaven's sake."

"I am," Alec assured him.

Alec saw an exit up ahead and decided he'd better take it. It was getting late, and they needed to find a mechanic at a gas station. The grinding of gears sounded even worse as they pulled out of the 125th Street exit onto a gritty, cement-lined boulevard in Harlem.

Henry frowned. "Where are you going?"

"I have to get someone to check on this clutch. I don't think we'll make it all the way home."

Henry said nothing.

"You want to break down on the road?" Alec asked, beginning to lose his patience.

He swung the van northward onto a wide avenue, still hoping to locate a nearby gas station with a garage. He finally found one after passing several blocks of sagging tenement buildings. Henry stayed with the van, looking annoyed, while Alec got out to see if he could find a mechanic.

A man inside the gas station office motioned to Alec to wait. He opened a door behind him and called, "Hey, Larry! Come on out here for a second."

From the shadows in the back of the garage emerged a heavyset man. He wore a grease-stained blue union suit with a zipper running up the middle. His eyelids looked heavy, as if he'd just woken up, but his eyes were clear and sharp. A patch sewn over the man's chest read LARRY.

Alec explained the situation with the gears. The mechanic pulled at his mustache thoughtfully. "Got a horse in there, huh?"

Alec nodded. The mechanic gazed at Alec, seeming to size him up. Alec stared back at the mechanic. Neither spoke for a few long moments. Finally, the big man said, "I suppose I could check her out."

Alec felt a wave of relief.

"But if you want me to drop everything I'm doing, it'll cost you extra."

Alec quickly assured the mechanic that he would pay him well for his time. Being stuck here in the city for the rest of the night wasn't a very appealing idea.

It didn't take Larry long to identify the source of the problem. "You got clutch troubles, chief," he called out from under the van.

"That's what I figured," Alec said. "Can you fix it?"

Larry slid his dolly out from under the van and stood up. "I'm not sure. Maybe. By tomorrow, for sure."

"But we have to get this colt home tonight. Couldn't you try?"

Larry snorted. "Oh, sure. Why not? It's only six o'clock and I was supposed to be home a half hour ago."

Despite the mechanic's snarling, Alec suspected he might not abandon them just yet. Something about the way Larry kept peeking into the van's rear window told Alec that the big man might be a race fan. Sure enough, after a little more coaxing, he set to work on the van, taking the clutch apart in record time. Soon the mechanic had replacement parts completely installed, minus one small disk which he didn't have on hand. Larry went into the office and dialed all his local suppliers, but without luck. Every place was closed.

"Now what?" Alec asked.

The mechanic stretched his long arms over his head and rubbed his back. "I'm no magician, chief. I can't make auto parts appear out of thin air."

Alec sighed. He certainly couldn't argue with the man's logic. He went to talk to Henry and found the old trainer slouched in a chair in the office, his fedora pulled down over his eyes. Henry was the only person Alec knew who could worry himself to sleep. Alec woke him up with a tap on the shoulder.

Immediately, Henry sat up. "Ready to go?" he asked.

"It looks like we have a problem." Alec told Henry about the missing part.

Henry threw up his hands. "Can't the guy rig something up temporarily? How about putting the old part back in?"

"No good." Alec shook his head. "He says we wouldn't get more than a mile before we broke down."

"Well, Storm can't stay here," Henry insisted. "That animal's too high-strung to stay cooped up in the van all night."

The two of them walked outside. Alec glanced around, trying to figure out what to do. Then he spotted a long panel truck plastered with electronics logos parked alongside the garage.

"What about that truck over there?" Alec asked.

Henry followed Alec's gaze and seemed to read his mind. "It's big enough, I guess."

"Sure, why not? Anything to get Storm back to the farm tonight. Hey, Larry!" Alec called.

The mechanic had gone inside to change his

25

clothes. When he emerged from the office again, dressed in jeans and a sweatshirt, Alec asked if he could rent the truck for a day.

Larry shrugged. "I don't know, chief. That truck belongs to my boss. He bought it at auction last week."

"Does it run?" Alec asked eagerly.

"Like a champion," Larry replied.

"Do you think you could call up your boss and ask him if we could rent it just for the night? We'd pay well. Otherwise I'm not sure what we could do. One way or the other, our horse can't stay in that van much longer."

The mechanic looked Alec squarely in the eye but didn't reply right away. Finally, he went inside and picked up the phone. Alec and Henry followed.

After Larry had dialed the number and explained the situation to his boss, he handed the phone to Alec. It took a fair amount of cajoling and wrangling, but in the end, Alec received permission to rent the truck. With a sigh of relief, Alec thanked Larry for his help and set to work beside Henry, transferring straw. Soon the two of them had rigged up a makeshift stall inside the truck that would be safe enough for Storm to make the trip home.

"We can't thank you enough, sir," Alec said

again, after Storm had been successfully loaded in and he and Henry were preparing to leave. "You're a lifesaver."

Larry nodded. "Have that truck back here by tomorrow afternoon. Your van should be ready by then."

"Great," Alec said, shaking the mechanic's hand.

"Give me a tip on the ponies someday, and we'll call it even," Larry told him with a wink.

Alec and Henry climbed into the truck. With a wave out the window, Alec turned onto the street and started up the avenue to find the next entrance onto the expressway. The streetlights were already on. Alec looked at his watch. It was after eight o'clock. He rubbed his neck, which was starting to feel sore. Boy, would he be glad to get home and sack out.

Just as they were about to turn up the ramp leading back onto the highway, Alec slowed the truck at a YIELD sign. Out of the corner of his eye, he spotted a shadow moving to his left. Moments later, a dark, hulking shape jumped up onto the truck's running board.

Alec jerked his head back. "What...?"

The door of the truck suddenly flew open and Alec was pulled roughly out of his seat. Immediately, he reached back to grab the keys from the ignition. They dropped to the floor of the cab. Henry reached down and scooped them up.

At first, Alec saw nothing but the gun pointed at his face. A hand grabbed him by the collar, pushing the gun barrel closer, and a voice garbled some words Alec had trouble understanding.

"Where's the keys, man?"

Alec played dumb. "Keys?"

"Hand over the keys!" The voice sounded young and nervous.

"They're on the floor," Alec said. "I dropped them."

The hijacker felt around the floor beneath the steering wheel, then looked over at Henry. "What's in your hands, Pops? Gimme those," he ordered. The old trainer didn't move.

"Come on, Henry," Alec said calmly. "He has a gun. Do as he says." Henry just stared at Alec, a hard expression on his face.

Alec kept his voice soft but firm. "Please, Henry. He has a gun."

Slowly, Henry handed over the keys. Another young thug, this one brandishing a tire iron, jerked open the passenger door. He pulled Henry out, backing the trainer up against the front fender.

"Move!" the kid with the gun said, kicking Alec

in the shins and pushing him around to the front of the truck. "You come through my neighborhood, you show some respect. Pay the toll."

His heart pounding, Alec turned around. For the first time, he managed to get a look at the punks. Both wore dark-colored New York Giants starter jackets, their faces hidden in shadow by hooded sweatshirts. From their general builds and the sound of their voices, Alec figured they were pretty young, probably no more than fifteen or sixteen.

"What is this?" demanded Henry.

"What's *this*, Pops?" The kid with the gun drew his free hand back as though to give Henry a slap in the face. Henry stiffened, his eyes glaring straight ahead.

The gunman threw his partner the keys. "Check the back." The kid with the tire iron jogged to the rear of the truck.

"You're making a mistake," Alec said. "This truck isn't carrying..."

Just then, Henry made a sudden move toward the young hood. The thug swung his pistol hard against the side of Henry's face.

Alec lunged for the attacker as Henry let out a groan and his knees buckled. He caught the kid in the chest and shoulder. The kid's mouth dropped open in surprise, and the gun fell from his hand.

The pistol went off, sending a bullet out into the night.

A fist hit Alec in the stomach, but he was too angry to feel anything. He swung back at his attacker with unbridled fury.

Alec heard footsteps running up alongside the truck as he continued to grapple with the thug. He barely saw the other hijacker rush up beside him, the raised tire iron in his hand. A dark blur cut through the headlights, and Alec felt himself zooming out into the sky, his vision blinded by a hundred exploding stars. Then came darkness.

CHAPTER FOUR

Lost Colt

"Mister," a voice said. "Are you all right? Mister?"

Alec opened his eyes. A plane of pavement slowly came into focus. His cheek was resting on cold, hard asphalt. "Come on, now," the voice went on. "That's it. Wake up."

Alec didn't move.

"Mister!" the voice called again, suddenly sounding loud and harsh. Alec blinked. The back of his head throbbed with each beat of his heart.

He turned his head and coughed. An upside-down face was hanging over him—a blurry, distorted cop face. The man started talking very fast, but Alec could understand only snatches of what he was saying. The ringing in his ears evened its pitch and slowly began to fade into the background.

"...Ambulance...That other guy...your grand-father?"

Henry! Alec struggled to get up. Waves of pain shot down his neck. Something hot and sticky was oozing down the side of his face. Blood. The cop put his hand on Alec's shoulder. "Take it easy, kid," he said. "The ambulance should be here any minute."

It all seemed to be happening in a dream. Flashing lights. The cop's concerned face. Hands helping him onto a stretcher and into an ambulance. The smell of rubbing alcohol and disinfectant, dark streets zooming by outside the window.

Alec closed his eyes for a moment. When he opened them again, he saw Henry lying on a stretcher beside him, a bandage wrapped around his head. All the color seemed to have been drained from Henry's face. He looked alarmingly old and frail. The sight jolted Alec awake. He sat up, grabbing the ice pack that had been placed behind his right ear, and tried to speak, but the shock of what had happened made the words choke in his throat.

Henry's eyes were wide open but his gaze seemed unfocused. Alec wished he could get his old friend to respond—to say anything. "Stay with me now, Henry," said Alec. "Come on. Hang in there." The EMS worker watched quietly. A baseball game was crackling softly on a portable radio. Alec turned to the worker with the thin mustache. "Can't you *do* something for him?"

The man shrugged. "Not till we get to the hospital. You're doing fine. Just try to keep your friend awake." His eyes held Alec's for a moment, then slid away. *This stuff doesn't even faze them,* Alec thought. *They must see it all the time.*

He gazed over at Henry, who was blinking up at the roof of the ambulance. "That's it, Henry. We're going to be there any minute now." Henry tried to say something, but the words came out thick and unintelligible.

Gingerly, Alec leaned over and wiped some grit from Henry's face. *How long had the two of them been lying there by the side of the road?* he wondered. It was a good thing that cop had stopped to help. Alec closed his eyes and saw the thug's gun in his face once again. He shuddered. What a nightmare.

Hadn't he tried to tell those creeps there was just a horse inside the truck? The hijackers must have seen the electronics company logos on the side of the truck and figured it was full of television sets and VCRs. If Henry hadn't been so impulsive, if he'd waited for the guy to check the back, maybe the hoods would have left them alone. On the other hand, those guys hadn't seemed like the types to leave empty-handed. Alec took a deep breath and let the air stream out slowly through his bloody nose. He and Henry were lucky that they hadn't wound up getting shot. And what had happened to Storm?

The ambulance siren finally stopped screaming as they came to a jarring stop at the emergency room entrance to the hospital. The ambulance door swung open with a bang.

Inside the emergency room, Alec watched as a nurse wearing a green scrub suit bent down over Henry to feel his pulse. Moments later, an orderly elbowed Alec to one side and wheeled Henry down a long, brightly lit corridor.

Another nurse led Alec back to his wheelchair and took him into an examination room. She tended to his bloody nose and the bump on his head, then gave him some aspirin. "The doctor will see you shortly," she said, and left.

An hour later, Alec sat beside his old friend's bed in a room full of high-tech machines with monitors, hoses, and gauges humming and buzzing and clicking. The air was cold and smelled artificially clean. Nurses hovered nearby, watching and waiting.

Henry began to regain consciousness after a few minutes. "What...the...? Where am I?"

"You're at the hospital, Henry," Alec said. "You

have a concussion, but the doctor says you're out of danger now."

Henry looked shrunken, his skin a peculiar gray pallor. He struggled to sit up. The nurse in the green scrub suit gently pushed him back down. "Not so fast," she told him. "Lie still now." The nurse kept an eye on the EEG and EKG machines that were monitoring Henry's brain waves and heart rate. Seeming satisfied with the readings, she stepped over to check on the patient in the next bed.

Henry turned his head on the pillow, a raw-looking bruise puffing the side of his face. "Alec, are you there?" he said hoarsely.

"Right beside you, Henry."

"We have to get back to the farm...So much work to do..."

Alec put his hand on Henry's arm to quiet him. "Don't worry, Henry. I'll take care of everything. You just do what the doctors tell you and concentrate on getting better."

The nurse attending the patient in the next bed glanced back at Alec. "Don't let him get too excited."

Henry grumbled and started to say something. The nurse narrowed her eyes and gave Alec a stern look. "You'd better go, young man," she said, walking briskly over to Alec and showing him the door.

"You can wait outside. And try to get some rest yourself, okay?"

Rest, thought Alec. *Oh, sure.* How could he rest with Henry here in the hospital and Black Storm in the hands of those two? Alec closed his eyes and took a deep breath. How could something like this even have happened? He thought about Storm and prayed that his horse was all right. He began to imagine horrible scenarios of what might happen to Storm. If the hijackers were smart enough to realize that the colt was a valuable racehorse, they could try to sell him out of state or even out of the country. Or they might stash him somewhere until the heat died down. Worst of all, they might even kill him.

Alec sat down in a plastic chair in the waiting room. What a day. First the spill at the track, and now this. He tried to quiet his nerves by focusing on what he was going to have to do. *I must stay calm,* he told himself. With any luck, there was a good chance that Storm would turn up on his own in the next day or so. The hijackers weren't international horse thieves. They were just kids looking for electronic goods to sell, not a horse. *But I can't just sit here doing nothing,* Alec thought.

He walked over to a pay phone and punched in the number of a sports reporter he knew from the track. Maybe the reporter could help get the word out about Storm. Alec figured that the first thing to do was to offer a reward and make as much noise as possible. Then they would just have to hope for the best. Right now, there was not much else to do except wait.

The next morning, after Alec had returned alone to the farm, he received word that the police had found the abandoned truck in Queens. Unfortunately, there was no sign of Black Storm.

After a few days, Henry was released from the hospital, and business slowly returned to normal at the farm. Every time the phone rang, Alec rushed to answer it, hoping for news about Storm.

The call finally came nearly a week after the hijacking. Alec was in the office at Hopeful Farm, trying to catch up on paperwork.

"Is this Alec Ramsay?" a deep voice asked.

"Who's this?" Alec answered, gripping the receiver tightly.

"The name's Matt Mason. I run a riding stable in Brooklyn. I think you might want to stop by here. A horse wandered onto my property the other day. I saw that story in the paper and thought he could be yours."

Alec had chased down five false leads already. He couldn't hide the skepticism in his voice as he asked for a description. It sounded like Storm, but then so had the others. "Just wandered out to Brooklyn all by himself, huh?"

The voice stiffened. "Listen, Mr. Ramsay, I'm trying to help *you* out. You want to come get your horse or not?"

Alec lowered the receiver and waited a moment to cool his nerves. The pressure of the past few days was getting to him. It was probably just another wild-goose chase, but...

"Okay," Alec said finally. "Are you going to be there for a while? I'll come take a look."

Mason gave Alec directions to his stable, way out on the outskirts of Brooklyn. Though Alec had grown up in nearby Flushing, the stable was in an area he had never been to before. After checking a map, he discovered that it was several miles from the place in Queens where the police had found the truck.

Henry walked stiffly into the office, muttering something about "shiftless good-for-nothings." The old trainer was still recovering from his injuries, but he was back at work, crankier than ever. He'd only been home a couple of days and he'd already fired the new groom. "Lazy," Henry had said, and that was the end of that.

Alec dashed past the trainer and jumped into the

cab of the horse van parked outside the office.

"Where do you think you're going?" Henry called after him. "We've got work to do."

"I'm heading into the city. We've got another call about Storm."

Henry gave him a sour look. "Humph."

Alec raised his eyebrows. "What's *that* supposed to mean?"

Henry just shrugged.

"Come on, Henry," said Alec. "Ever since the hijacking, you've been acting as if you blamed Storm for what happened."

"Don't be ridiculous, Alec," Henry snapped. "I'm telling you, you should let the police handle this whole thing."

"And in the meantime, I'm supposed to just forget about my horse?"

"*Your* horse? Black Storm belongs to Hopeful Farm, not you. And don't you forget it. What about the Black? And that barn full of two-year-olds? We have plenty of other horses to worry about, Alec. Animals that are worth a lot more to us than Storm."

There was no denying that, Alec had to admit. In pure monetary terms, Black Storm was one of the least valuable horses at the farm. Alec decided he'd better change the subject, fast. "Has anyone called about the groom job yet?"

"No. Someone will."

"All right, then," Alec said. "So take it easy, will you? Remember what the doctor said."

Henry grunted again, dismissing Alec with a wave of his hand. Alec watched as the bowlegged old trainer headed back into the barn.

"Whew," Alec said under his breath. He started the van's motor, made a quick U-turn, and roared out the driveway. Whatever happened, one thing was for sure. The way Henry felt about Storm, finding the colt and keeping him would be two entirely different problems to solve.

CHAPTER FIVE

———— ❧ ❧ ————

An Unexpected Discovery

Matt Mason's neighborhood was a melting pot of cultures in collision. Fifty years earlier it had been filled with immigrants from Italy, Ireland, and Eastern Europe. Later, Chinese immigrants had settled there, as well as blacks, Latinos, and East Indians. As he drove through the crowded streets, Alec figured that half the people on the planet were probably represented in this one small section of Brooklyn.

At each stoplight, Alec heard a montage of different languages. Street vendors hawked watches, perfumes, videocassette tapes, and a thousand other wares. Passersby gathered in front of an electronics store, watching a music video on a stack of TV monitors in the display window. Pedestrians ignored crossing lights and dodged the congested, stop-and-go traffic.

A siren whooped down a side street. Alec figured it could have belonged to a fire truck, ambulance, or cop car. It didn't really matter—no one seemed overly concerned. Sirens were part of the environment here, like wind in the trees or waves at the beach.

Alec negotiated the van past a line of taxis double-parked outside a takeout restaurant. Consulting the directions he'd taken down over the phone, he began to count the traffic lights, following Gunnery Street into an industrial area of warehouses, loading docks, and abandoned factories. The old lumberyard that Mason had told him to keep an eye out for was up ahead on the right. A sudden, strong whiff of horse manure blew through the open window, letting Alec know that he was on the right track.

The pockmarked, semi-paved driveway leading to the stables soon gave way to dirt, winding past the boarded-up lumberyard office and around to the back. A rooster and some chickens scurried past, squawking loudly. Around the corner of the crumbling old building, Alec could see two horse sheds. A small paddock stood to one side of the yard. Inside, a worn-looking bay mare with a clean shiny coat waited patiently. A stocky man outfitted in faded denim and a cowboy hat was lifting a small red-haired girl up into the saddle. A handful of kids hung on the railing to watch. *Riding lessons,* Alec realized.

Adjacent to the paddock was a larger corral, its fencing constructed of scrap wood. Additional fencing bounded the perimeter of the abandoned lumberyard. All of the sheds and corrals were built of recycled wood, aluminum siding, or other scavenged materials. A milk goat tied up beside one of the sheds calmly sniffed the ground at her feet. A police siren crackled a few times, then began to wail somewhere off in the neighborhood.

Horses? Goats? Chickens? In Brooklyn? Why not? Alec knew better than to be too surprised by anything in New York City. His thoughts flashed back to Hopeful Farm, with its modern barns and miles of wide green pastures and fields. Whoever this Matt Mason was, Alec thought, he had to admire the guy's ingenuity for turning an abandoned lumberyard into a working stable.

From the paddock, the man waved his cowboy hat at Alec and strode over to the van. His build was that of a slightly-over-the-hill prizefighter, and his smiling eyes were set wide apart in a large, smooth face. His head was shaved bald.

"You're Alec Ramsay?"

Alec nodded.

"Thought so. I've seen you race, man. You and

the Black at Belmont last year, the time you beat Bandolero."

Alec flashed a smile and got out of the van. The warm, dry hand that grasped Alec's was callused and powerful. "It's a real pleasure meeting you," the big man said. "Welcome to East Gunnery Community Stables."

"Thanks. You must be Mr. Mason," Alec said.

"Call me Mace," the cowboy said. He waved back to the kids in the paddock. "That's one of my riding classes."

Alec nodded, but he couldn't help feeling a little impatient. "So what's the story, Mace? A horse that looks like mine just turned up here all on his own?"

"That's about the size of it," Mace replied. "Showed up the other morning when I came out to give the other horses their morning feed."

"You're pretty sure the colt is Black Storm?" Alec asked.

Mason snorted. "Unless there happens to be more than one big black three-year-old colt with a silver blaze wandering through the neighborhood these days."

"Any idea who had him before he found his way here?"

"Couldn't say," the stable owner answered. "There are a lot of crazy kids around here who might have gotten their hands on him. I guess whoever it was couldn't figure out what else to do with him, so they left the colt here. Everyone in the neighborhood knows about my stable."

Alec nodded slowly, trying to place the man's accent. It sounded Southern, but he couldn't be sure. There was something cultured and polished about it, like a college professor's, but with a street wise edge.

"If you don't mind my asking," Alec said, "why did it take you so long to call? You said the colt has been here for days."

Mace read the suspicion in Alec's eyes and pursed his lips. "I saw the news reports," he said, shrugging. "But the only phone number they gave was for a police station. I wanted to talk with you directly, not with some detective. That's the last thing I need, a bunch of cops poking around here. I would have called sooner, but I had to find the number of your stable and that took a while."

Alec figured he'd let the stable owner's explanation slide. Maybe Mace was covering up for someone, but it could also be true that he just hadn't wanted to get overly involved in the whole situation.

"So where's Storm now?" Alec asked eagerly. He nodded toward the horse shed. "In there?"

"Nah. One of the kids took him for a ride about an hour ago. That colt of yours sure can get himself worked up. Creo thought a little exercise might cool him off."

Alec raised his eyebrows. Go for a ride? What in the world was Mace talking about? "Uh, where?" he asked. "On the street? There aren't any parks near here, are there?"

"They were headed over to North Washington, I think."

"But isn't that over a mile away?" Alec was really beginning to lose his patience now.

"Just about. Unless they used the freeway."

Alec's mouth dropped open. "There's a freeway around here?"

Mace read Alec's look of bewilderment and smiled. "Just the East-West Freeway. Come on, I'll show you," he offered. He motioned to Alec and started walking toward the sheds.

Alec was dumbfounded, but he followed the stable owner anyway. *What am I getting myself into?* he wondered. *Does this guy mean the Brooklyn-Queens Expressway?*

"I know what you're thinking, Mr. Ramsay. It may not be legal to ride on the freeway. Then again, it may not be legal to ride on the city streets, either."

Alec just stared at the stable owner, still confused. Mace chuckled and put a hand on Alec's shoulder. "Don't panic, kid. There aren't any cars on the

East-West. The city finished building only part of it. They ran out of funding last year. It's supposed to run past here and all the way to Queens, when they get through with it. *If* they get through with it, rather."

Alec still found the whole idea hard to believe. "But is it really safe to ride there?"

Mace shrugged. "Sure. Most of it isn't even paved. It's just soft dirt and grass, perfect for riding."

Alec looked away and rolled his eyes. New York. What a city. There was no place like it.

A few minutes later, Alec and the stable owner rode out of the lumberyard driveway and onto the street. Mace led the way on a rangy bay filly. Alec followed on one of the stable's riding horses. Tina was a sturdy old chestnut mare who probably could have walked past an exploding bomb without flinching. She reminded Alec of a veteran grade school teacher who had weathered decades of rambunctious students and lived to tell the tale.

The horses crossed the street and filed past a corner bodega, a used furniture store, and a beauty salon. They walked by tenement buildings with boarded windows and a record shop blaring a pulsating merengue beat. It wasn't as crowded as some of the avenues, but it was busy enough to spook most horses. Again he had to wonder if the horse Mace had called about could really be Black Storm. It was hard to picture hotheaded Storm trotting calmly by all this traffic and noise. Alec knew that even he, a professional jockey and Storm's regular rider, would have his hands full trying to handle him.

Mace's filly expertly picked her way between parked cars and neighborhood traffic as calmly as if she were passing bushes and trees on a park trail. Alec's mare seemed immune to the commotion on the streets as well, serenely tagging along behind Mace's filly.

Some of the people on the sidewalk glanced their way, but no one seemed very surprised to see them. Every few feet, someone waved a greeting to Mace or dished out a friendly insult.

As they crossed a busy intersection, Alec saw a ramp leading up to the elevated portion of the empty unfinished freeway. Mason edged around the wooden barricade that blocked the ramp entrance, and Alec pulled up beside him.

Is this some kind of wild-goose chase? Alec wondered. Mace's description of the horse he'd found had sounded a lot like Storm. But Alec still couldn't help feeling skeptical.

The horses moved up the ramp and onto the unpaved stretch of road above the streets. "The community let us take this place over, more or less," Mace said. "We maintain it, keep it clean. The city's been looking the other way for the time being." They walked their horses another hundred yards until he announced, "I think I see them. Looks like they're headed this way."

Alec gazed in the direction Mace was pointing. A small dot on the distant span of deserted highway was growing larger as a horse and rider sprinted toward them. The rider rocked back and forth in his seat with all the poise of a pro. The sound of the approaching hoofs gradually grew louder, marking a strict staccato rhythm. The form of horse and rider was smooth and flawless. As they raced closer, Alec realized that the horse was without a doubt Black Storm.

Alec felt an instant, overwhelming wave of relief as the flying colt drew down upon them. The person in the saddle was hand-riding Storm, his stirrups hiked up high in racing fashion. Storm thundered ahead without any apparent direction from the reins. Horse and rider moved effortlessly together, as if of one fluid mind.

Mace smiled proudly. "Not bad, huh? The kid's a natural."

Alec still couldn't believe the young rider was keeping Storm in hand so well. "Not bad at all. What did you say his name was?"

"Creo Chase."

"I guess it didn't take him long to get through to Storm," said Alec. "And that colt's quite a handful, believe me."

"I've known Creo from day one. I know all his people. His dad's from Brooklyn. His mother's family emigrated from the West Indies about fifteen years ago. They're all horse people. We had Creo in a saddle before he could walk."

"Really?" asked Alec. "You mean here?"

"Sure," Mace replied. "There have been stables in this neighborhood for years. Ours is the only one left."

Alec shook his head. "This is all news to me."

Mace just laughed and waved Creo in. As Black Storm drew closer, Alec dismounted and scrutinized the colt's every move. He showed no signs of being injured, stiff, or sore. Alec watched as Creo pulled Storm to a stop and jumped off, his face flushed from the ride.

Creo was about fifteen, Alec's size with short, thick hair and dark brown skin. He wore a purple T-shirt, baggy jeans, and black high-top sneakers. The faintest beginnings of a goatee darkened his chin, and a tiny gold earring pierced his left ear.

Alec called to the colt, who acknowledged him with a long, drawn-out whinny. Storm jerked his head and thrashed his tail. When the colt had finished showing off, Alec went over and wrapped his arms around Storm's neck. "So, what happened to you, fella?" Gently, he leaned against the horse. Storm snorted but allowed Alec to scratch his ears. "Boy, if you could only talk…"

"Don't worry," Creo spoke up. "He's okay."

"It sure looks like it," Alec said. It was true. The colt seemed fine. His eyes shone brightly and his breathing was even, as if the ride hadn't even fazed him.

Alec turned to Creo. "I can't believe Storm ran for you like that. He's usually a little crazy, even for me. You made it look easy."

Creo flushed at the praise, but his words rushed out excitedly. "Man, can he go! I've always wanted to ride a horse like this one. I've dreamed about it for years. Maybe he could tell."

"Maybe so." Alec chuckled and shook his head, still feeling a bit overwhelmed by the whole scene. He pulled a piece of carrot from his jacket pocket and held it out to Storm. He gently rubbed the colt's neck as Storm chomped away on the carrot.

Mace reined his horse around. "Well, let's get a move on." Creo's green eyes held a hint of sadness as he turned the reins over to Alec.

Alec looked at Creo, then at Storm, then back at Creo. *I should let the kid enjoy one last ride,* he thought. *What could it hurt?* He could tell that the kid was dying to get back in the saddle of his dream horse again. "I'll stick with Buttercup here," Alec told him. "You can ride Storm back to the stable if you want."

Creo's eyes lit up again. "Yeah? All right!" In one quick hop, he was back in the saddle.

Storm continued to behave himself, and together the three riders started back to the ramp that led down to the street. Alec turned to Creo. "That's some training track the city built for you up here."

"Yeah," Creo answered. "I hope they never finish paving it over."

"Where'd you learn to ride like that?"

"Right here." He grinned and nodded to Mace. "This guy is a great teacher."

Mace shrugged. "I just helped to get you started. His uncle works up at Aqueduct as a groom," he added to Alec.

That makes sense, Alec thought. He looked at Creo. "So you've been hanging around the backside, huh?"

"Helping out some."

"Have a galloping license?"

"Yeah," Creo answered proudly. "One of the trainers Uncle Ike works for helped me get it."

Alec smiled. "Getting any races?"

"Not yet." Creo sounded disappointed. "A few workouts once in a while, nothing regular. It's been hard with school and all. Maybe this summer." Alec hid a smile. The kid was trying to sound matter-of-fact in his shop talk.

"This time of year it's tough for a new face to get a break," Alec said. "A lot of the heavies are in town for the season. How old are you, anyway?"

"Sixteen."

Alec squinted, giving Creo a critical look. More like fourteen or fifteen, he guessed. Sixteen was the legal age to get a galloping license, so maybe that was just the kid's story.

Creo was already on the big side for a jockey, somewhere around five foot two or three. On the other hand, so was Alec. But if the kid grew any taller, his shot at making it as a jockey was a million to one. *No point in dashing the kid's dreams,* Alec thought. *There was always hope.* "You'll get your chance," he said. "Don't give up."

Creo gave him a thumbs-up. "That's my motto. Never say die."

As they rode slowly back to the stable, Creo asked Alec questions about the horses at Hopeful Farm and some of the races he'd seen Alec ride. He was no starry-eyed fan, though. His questions were cool and straightforward. Alec answered the questions automatically, listening with one ear to the rush of traffic. Every now and then he glanced up at the stark outlines of the surrounding public housing towers. This would be a tough place for a kid to live.

When they arrived back at the stable, a few of the students from the riding class were still there. A dark-haired girl wearing glasses and a red shirt was cleaning tack with saddle soap and a damp sponge. A boy who looked like her brother was spreading fresh straw on the floor inside one of the stalls. Two sleepy-looking mares and a pony cropped grass along the edge of the paddock.

Mace waved toward his students. "These kids learn a lot more here than riding," he said to Alec. "If they want to ride, I tell them they have to know how to take care of the horses first. They have to *earn* the chance to ride."

Alec nodded. "It must be great to have the extra hands, too. Hopeful Farm should look this clean." He wasn't kidding, either. Mace's stable may have been built out of recycled signs and cracked plywood, but the place was well kept. The grounds were raked and the animals were neatly groomed and fit. Everything was in its place.

An Unexpected Discovery

"Hey, if you ever need any extra help at the track or upstate, let me know," Creo said as he dismounted and gave Storm an affectionate slap on the neck. Then he bent over and began fiddling with the girth strap on the colt's saddle.

Alec watched him for a moment. The kid certainly seemed to know what he was doing around horses—at least around Storm, and that was saying something. Maybe...

"As a matter of fact," Alec said slowly, "we just lost a barn hand the other day. We could use some help. We're way up in Millville, though."

Creo pulled the saddle from the colt's back, then turned and leveled his gaze at Alec. "Mr. Ramsay, I'd move to Alaska to get a chance to work at Hopeful Farm. Seriously!"

Alec hesitated. What would Henry say? But they *did* need help. "The season is coming up at Saratoga," he said finally. "We're going to be busy. It's hard work."

"I can step up. Just give me a chance." Creo's voice was eager, practically pleading.

"Can you get a recommendation?" Alec asked.

"Sure. I know at least two trainers at Aqueduct who will put in a good word for me."

Alec nodded. He knew that he would have to

talk to Henry about this first before making any decisions. But the kid seemed like a hard worker. He might be just the ticket.

"Come up and see us," Alec said. "We might be able to work something out."

A wide grin spread across Creo's face. "You mean it? But where could I stay?" he asked breathlessly.

"You could bunk in the barn. There's space. The main thing is, you'd have to be ready right away. We need someone now."

"School's over," Creo said. "I'm ready."

"And don't forget your folks," Alec added. "It has to be okay with them, of course."

"They'll be fine with it, I'm sure," Creo said. He and Alec shook hands, and Alec gave him a piece of paper with his name and Hopeful Farm's address and phone number. The kid looked at the paper as if it were a hundred dollar bill he'd just found on the sidewalk. "I don't know how to thank you, Mr. Ramsay," he said.

Alec laughed. "Call me Alec, okay? I'm only a few years older than you."

Creo turned to Mace, his face shining. The Brooklyn cowboy just smiled and put out his hand to Creo for a low five. The two of them slapped palms.

Alec backed the van around, and Creo gave him

a hand loading Storm. The colt balked a few times, but they finally managed to coax the temperamental horse inside. Before he left, Alec handed Mace a check for a thousand dollars, the reward he'd offered for finding Storm.

Mace hesitated. For a moment, Alec thought he might be too proud to accept it. "Finances are always tight around here," Mace said finally, slipping the check into a pocket in his denim jacket. "It costs money to keep horses in the city, same as in the country. This will sure help. Thank you. The kids will appreciate it."

After calling Henry to give him the good news, Alec got back into the van, feeling extremely pleased. The reward money would be well spent. He may have found some good barn help. And best of all, he'd found Storm. Maybe now he could finally put the terrible night of the hijacking behind him.

CHAPTER SIX

The Black

Alec cautiously guided the van back through the crowded neighborhood streets, avoiding potholes and jaywalkers. Someone in a car behind him honked loudly. *Everybody's in such a hurry here in the city,* Alec thought. He couldn't wait to get out of there, back to where there was room to breathe.

Once he pulled onto the New York State Thruway, Alec finally started to relax. Storm was safe. Now he could focus again on running the farm—and racing. Two hours later, he was turning down the lane leading toward home and the rolling fields of Hopeful Farm.

He gazed out at the miles of fence, dozens of paddocks, sheds, and barns. *I'm lucky to live here,* he thought. Everything at Hopeful Farm was dedicated to raising the finest possible racehorses. There was no place he'd rather be. But sometimes the feeling of responsibility weighed heavily on his shoulders. The cost of running the farm was unbelievable. No matter how many races their horses won, Hopeful Farm seemed to be perpetually in debt, usually about two checks ahead of bankruptcy.

Alec tried to put that thought out of his mind. The farm was a small business like any other, with Alec's parents and Henry Dailey as the owners. Alec's official position was stable rider, and he took his job at Hopeful Farm very seriously. He saddle-broke the yearlings, giving them their first tastes of carrying a rider on their backs. He also assisted Henry in the training and, with his parents off visiting relatives in California, he was managing more and more of the day-to-day office work as well.

Alec unloaded Storm and turned him out into a field to cool off. Storm charged away, jigging left and right, eager to shake off the ride.

Just then, Henry came out of the training barn, zeroing his sights on Storm. He put down the clipboard he was holding and walked over to Alec, still watching the colt.

Alec figured Henry would be happy to see Storm back at the farm, but the trainer's expression was deadpan. There was no guessing what Henry was thinking with *that* look ironed onto his face.

"So you found him in Brooklyn, huh?" Henry said as he came up. The colt was cantering across the field now, his high-flying tail swishing back and forth. "Did they catch the punks who took him?"

"No," Alec replied. "The man who found him, his name's Mason. He said Storm just showed up. He runs this amazing little stable. You should see it, Henry, right in the middle of Brooklyn."

Henry raised his eyebrows. "Oh, yeah? Where?"

"It's a boarded-up lumberyard in Gunnery."

Henry slowly digested that information. He pushed back his fedora and rubbed the lump on his head, muttering something under his breath. Then his gaze caught Storm again and he watched the colt silently for a few moments. A hint of distant amusement lightened his poker face.

"The little monster doesn't seem any the worse for wear. Look at him out there, spinning around like a top."

Storm was putting on a real show, dancing around in the middle of the field. The colt squealed a few times to whoever might be listening, then burst into another fit of bucking and playing.

Henry turned serious again. "That animal might not have turned out so bad if his dam had been bred for the track," he said, his voice raspy. "But the

Ghost was trained as a circus performer. No one ever intended her to race. I guess it's not so surprising her foal turned out like he did." Henry shook his head. "How I ever let you talk me into that mare just because she was in foal to the Black, I'll never understand."

There was no denying that Storm's breeding was unusual, Alec knew. Yet that didn't mean it made sense to dismiss the colt as a potential racehorse, especially with the Black for a sire.

"The Ghost was a fantastic animal," Alec argued. "You saw her performance that night at Madison Square Garden. How many other horses could have put on a show like that, without a rider and with only voice commands to guide her?"

The recollection barely read on Henry's hard face. "I remember. I'll never forget that show, either." He sounded tired, but his words were firm. "You know the truth as well as I do. Storm just doesn't fit in here at Hopeful Farm. Not as a sprinter. Not as a distance runner. Not even as a jumper."

"Come on, Henry!" Alec persisted. "Look at him. He's…"

"What did I just say?" Henry cut in sharply. "The Ghost never raced, Alec. And Storm…Well, you know what *he's* like."

"But he's the Black's colt, too."

Henry shrugged. "Can't deny that."

"I want to get him back in training as soon as I can," Alec said. "Maybe tomorrow."

Henry sighed. "Why don't you jump one of the other horses, one who isn't so belligerent?"

"Because Max Dwyer said Storm was a natural-born steeplechaser," Alec shot back. "And I have a gut feeling he's right. Remember last year, that day when Storm broke away from me and started taking those jumps in the upper pasture all by himself? How often have you seen a horse without a rider jump hedges just for the fun of it? They usually swerve around."

"What does that prove?" Henry asked. "The horse is a nut case? We already know that."

"We've been through all this a million times, Henry. I'll work Storm on my own time if I have to."

"I'm in charge of the training program around here," Henry said. "Of *all* the stock, understand? This is a team. This is a system. We're not free-lancers, kid."

Alec dropped his head slightly. "I know, Henry."

Henry gave Alec another hard look. Deep grooves ran from the wings of his nose to the corners of his mouth. He puffed his cheeks and blew air through his partly opened lips. Then, adjusting his fedora, the old trainer gave a slight shrug. "If that's the way you feel, fine. I won't stand in your way. Just don't forget who'll be paying the bills around here for the next year or so. The two-year-olds in that training barn, not Black Storm."

Henry gazed at Alec with an expression that said "What are you waiting around here for?" Alec took the hint and sprinted over to the training barn to check who was on the exercise sheet for the rest of the day. A barn full of horses needed exercising.

These little blowups between him and Henry were becoming more frequent, Alec mused. And this time Henry was making the situation clear: When it came to the horses at Hopeful Farm, he was the boss.

Alec stepped into the training barn and checked the daybook on the wall outside the tack room. Even though he loved the world of Hopeful Farm, sometimes he couldn't help wondering if there wasn't more to life. Every so often he wished he could just take the Black and disappear for a while. Maybe he could find some open country out west and get lost for a few weeks. *Keep dreaming,* Alec told himself. Horse racing wasn't just a way to earn a living. It was a way of life, twenty-four hours a day, seven days a week.

Alec glanced about him, and a pang of guilt shivered through his chest. Was Henry right? Had he been neglecting his job? The training schedule was definitely out of whack now, since he had been off tracking down leads on Storm for the past week. Henry's firing of the new groom hadn't helped matters, either. Deb, the head groom, did his best, but one barn hand couldn't handle all the chores at Hopeful Farm. They needed help—and soon.

Alec suddenly remembered Creo, wondering whether the kid was really as eager for work as he'd sounded. He wasn't sure if he wanted to mention anything about Creo to Henry just now, especially with the mood Henry was in. It was time to get to work.

Just before sunset, after Alec had worked the last two-year-old scheduled for the day, he stepped into the office to tackle a stack of bills. After a while, though, his concentration began to drift as the dying afternoon light streaked through the office window. He sorted out the most urgent bills and pushed the remaining ones back into the pile, promising himself that he would finish them all after dinner. It was too late to catch the afternoon mail pickup, anyway. He got up and walked outside, gathering a saddle and bridle from the tack room. Then he hurried off to find the Black.

The stallion stood by a fence at the far end of his pasture, watching the horses in the next field. It made

Alec feel good just to see the Black at the farm instead of the track. The Black was a lover of freedom. He thrived on blowing wind and green grass. Born to the wild, the Black could never be confined for long.

Alec whistled to him, but the stallion kept his gaze focused on the other horses. Alec whistled again. The Black's tail stirred briefly. Alec gave a wry smile. "Nice to see you, too," he called. He slipped through the fence slats and started out across the grass.

Midway across the field, he whistled again. This time the Black turned to acknowledge him. The stallion moved slowly away from the fence, his head down, a brooding expression on his face. His step was long and graceful, even at a walk. That gave him the long stride typical of the great stretch runners, masters of the classic Belmont move: wide around the last turn and past the field, pushing the competition out of the way.

People who love their horses are all alike, Alec thought. Each believed his own horse was the fastest, bravest, strongest, kindest, and smartest. For Alec, there was little doubt about the Black. In conformation, the stallion's strength and beauty surpassed anything he had ever seen.

The Black's scent grew stronger as he drew

closer, then came to a halt beside Alec. Alec gently pressed his forearm against the horse's chest, and the Black bobbed his head. Hot breath blew threw Alec's hair. Then the stallion bent his neck to touch Alec's shoulder with his muzzle. Alec leaned against the Black. "Be still," he told him.

After a moment, the Black back-stepped a few paces, watching Alec expectantly. As the stallion moved, his tremendous muscles bunched and rolled under his skin. A minute passed, but Alec didn't say a word. He simply stood there, watching. It was always startling to see the Black up close. Sometimes he forgot how big the stallion really was.

Finally, Alec slipped the bridle over the Black's head. The stallion feigned rebellion. He pawed the ground, then half reared, his mane flying and his eyes wide. Alec waited patiently until the Black finished his performance. Then, with a hand on the stallion's withers, he vaulted into the saddle.

Immediately, everything fell into place. Alec felt complete, every part in balance. And he knew the Black felt more than the weight of his body. The Black felt his touch, his knowledge and understanding, their whole history together.

Once again Alec recalled their first ride together, a wild dash across a deserted stretch of beach on a far-off Mediterranean island. Other images continued to flash through his mind, memories of spectacular races and fantastic adventures. Through it all, one fact remained the same: how much simpler and sweeter the world always seemed from up on the Black.

"Come on, Black," said Alec, slapping the stallion's neck. "Let's go."

They followed the fence to the gate. Once past it, the stallion broke out into a canter, then a gallop, carrying Alec toward the open fields above Hopeful Farm. The Black's strides lengthened, drawing the stallion into a sweeping turn. In the distance, Alec saw the roll of the country—the rising lines of hills, his own house, the barns of Hopeful Farm, and the long driveway lined with poplars that ran out to the county road.

The Black slowed to a trot as they passed through a broken-down rail fence. They rode on through another long field, crossing a little sunken creek that flowed past blackberry and raspberry brambles. The trail was like a tunnel in places, so overgrown that Alec had to duck several times to avoid being hit by the branches. It was the only passable trail to the place he knew they were going: the stream-fed pond at the edge of the dense woods that bordered Hopeful Farm.

The field that surrounded the pond was wide

and empty. In the middle of the field were the remains of an old apple tree that had been struck by lightning two years before. As they drew near the tree, Alec dismounted with a quick swing of his legs and untacked the Black. Then he turned the stallion loose.

Alec watched the fading sunlight tint the sky, the fields, the trees. It even blushed the light film of sweat slicking the Black's coat. The thud of hoofs softened and the sweaty smell of the Black faded with the fresh wind as he trotted down to the pond. Alec sat on a patch of moss, leaning his back against the fallen part of the tree. Above him, the wind rattled the leaves in the half that was still standing.

Every so often, Alec needed this special time. If only for a short while, he wanted to forget about running the farm, about racing and making money. He simply wanted to relax and enjoy where he was at the moment—alone with the Black.

CHAPTER SEVEN

Magic Touch

The next few days were nonstop work for Alec, from five-thirty in the morning until well into the night. Aside from exercising the twelve horses in training—nine of them two-year-olds needing special care—he continued to help out in the barn and the office. He and Henry didn't even talk about Storm. It was probably best to let the subject slide for a while, Alec decided. Besides, there was just too much else to do.

Alec put extra effort into the workouts, trying to follow Henry's instructions to the letter. If Henry wanted two furlongs in twenty-six seconds, that was what he got. And, Alec knew, that was the way it should be, anyway. Alec had always watched and learned from Henry. Henry's methods were classic old school. He was a master trainer, guided by intelligence, intuition, and decades of experience.

The horses were special, too. Each one of them required a different touch. Some were temperamental, some easygoing, some fast learners, some not. As the regular rider for the stable, Alec was responsible for detecting the many subtle habits, particularly correctable ones, that only a regular rider could recognize. That information he passed on directly to Henry.

Deb, the head groom, was also an integral part of the training process. He'd been a racetracker almost as long as Henry. No one knew the stock at Hopeful Farm better than old Deb, ever-present in his blue denim overalls, his squinting eyes watchful, his face the color of worn saddle leather. He spent more time than anyone with the horses in the training barn, rubbing them down, feeding them, and consoling them late at night. Often he would be the first to detect some very slight change in a horse's temperament.

Alec came in from the last workout of the day on a two-year-old filly named Black Wind. He tethered her to the mechanical hot walker to cool out for twenty minutes. The circular turnstile, its arms designed to steadily rotate counterclockwise, looked as though it belonged on a playground, a combination swing set and merry-go-round. Black Wind jostled the tether, then slowly moved with it.

Ordinarily, they didn't use the mechanical hot walker. At Hopeful Farm, the job of walking "hots"—the horses just coming off the track—usually fell to one of the grooms. Walking a hot horse for thirty minutes or so after a workout was a simple but all-important part of a racehorse's daily routine. It gave the horse time to wind down from his exercise session before returning to his stall.

These days, without a second groom, they didn't have much choice but to use the mechanical hot walker. Henry hated the machine. Too many things can go wrong, he always said, especially with a volatile horse. A few years earlier, a stakes-winning mare in California had blinded herself in one eye after rearing up and striking her face on a metal joint. The newer models, like the one at Hopeful Farm, were safer, but Henry still distrusted them—even with the most docile horses. The only reason they'd bought the machine was for emergency backup.

Maybe, with a bit of luck, they wouldn't need to use the machine for much longer. Last night, Creo Chase, the kid from Brooklyn, had called and made an appointment for a job interview at the farm. He seemed like a good candidate to Alec, but as always, Henry would have the final say. As desperately as they needed help, Henry was extremely particular. He wouldn't hire the first guy who walked in off the street. He'd already turned down three applicants. Creo might get a break if he caught Henry in a good mood.

Black Wind continued pacing around the worn circular path. Alec watched her move, his critical eyes studying her body. He listened to the fall of each hoof and the air going in and out her nostrils in big, slow breaths.

At one point during the workout, she had felt a bit off-stride. Alec scratched his chin pensively, wondering if that inconsistency might signify some developing problem. He wished he could spend time cooling her out himself, but he needed to go to town and he was already running late.

Alec called over to Deb to keep an eye on the filly. The old groom was sitting on a bench, cleaning riding equipment. He was knee-deep in exercise saddles, reins, bits and blinkers. As he jogged off toward the pickup, Alec saw Henry in one of the paddocks, working a two-year-old on a longe line. With soft, encouraging words, he was coaxing the filly to trot around him in wide circles at the end of the long canvas rein.

It was almost sundown when Alec returned from town two hours later. He backed the pickup around to the training barn to unload the sacks of special feed he'd ordered. He hopped out of the truck and started to grapple with one of the heavy sacks. Just as he was about to heave it up onto his shoulder, a voice called from behind, "Hey, let me help you with that."

Alec turned and nearly dropped the sack. Creo Chase was standing there in the driveway, grinning at him. The kid was wearing work clothes and a Yankees baseball cap. Henry came around the side of the barn and said to Alec, "He came right after you left. I let him groom one of the colts. He did a good job."

Alec nodded. "I'm sure he did." Creo was already tugging at a feed sack. "So how'd you get here, anyway?" Alec asked.

"By train. Then bus. Then by foot."

"You *walked* here?" Alec was amazed.

"Only a couple miles."

"Pretty impressive," Alec said, chuckling. No doubt the effort Creo had made to reach Hopeful Farm impressed Henry, too.

"We'll give the kid here a try," said Henry. "At least until we can find some professional help."

"I don't care if it's just for one day," Creo said eagerly. "This place is so fine. Even the horses smell different here."

"Well, I don't know about that," Alec said. "But

okay, then, help me finish unloading this feed. I'll show you where it goes."

Twenty minutes later, after Alec and Creo had stored the supplies from the truck, Alec turned the new barn help over to Deb. Henry ducked his head into the office, where Alec was beginning to file away the sales receipts.

The trainer jerked his thumb toward the door. "Kid says his uncle works for Duane Muni over at Belmont. Claims he's been hanging out down there."

"Did he tell you he had his galloping license?" Alec asked.

Henry snorted. "Yeah. And he can keep it in his pocket. Right now we have to get this barn back into shape."

Creo adapted quickly to life at Hopeful Farm. With his help, Alec and Deb began to tackle the jobs that had been stacking up over the past few weeks. Saddles and bridles were checked for frayed stitching. Blankets, fly sheets, rain slickers, and wool coolers were shaken out, cleaned, and refolded. Shipping bandages were washed, dried, and rerolled.

Creo was eager to make a good impression. He went about his chores with enthusiasm, no matter what the job. He walked hots, mucked out stalls, and washed, groomed, and fed the horses.

He also passed all the little tests that Deb and Henry set before him. When Deb intentionally left halters on a pair of two-year-olds, Creo carefully removed the headgear before turning the horses loose in their pasture. He always opened gates and stall doors extra-wide for the horses, avoiding the potentially deadly situation of a horse trying to lunge through a narrow opening and jamming its hindquarters between gate and fencepost.

Henry watched Creo work and nodded with approval. "The kid seems to know his way around a horse barn, all right," he muttered to Alec one afternoon. "Now, if I could just understand why he wears that ridiculous earring. What does he think he is, some sort of pirate?"

Alec laughed. "Come on, Henry. Guys have been wearing earrings for ages. Man, are you out of it."

Henry shook his head in bemused disbelief. "What's next?"

"Maybe a tattoo. I was thinking of getting one myself." Alec grinned at the stunned look on Henry's face. "Just kidding, Henry. But, hey, what does any of that matter, as long as Creo handles our horses correctly?"

Henry couldn't argue with that. From then on, little more was said on the subject of tattoos and earrings.

Once the training schedule was more or less back to normal, Henry's mood improved considerably. Luke Stedman, a big-time Florida-based trainer, had called and said he would be stopping by to look at some stock. That really cheered Henry up. Stedman represented a number of wealthy businessmen, mainly oil sheiks and shipping magnates, who were investing in horses. Last summer he had arranged to buy two Hopeful Farm fillies. One of them, Nite Thyme, had gone on to become a stakes-winning champion.

Even Storm seemed to lose some of his obstinacy over the next few days. Alec convinced Henry to let him set up some low hurdles on the training track and give the colt a workout. Storm ran well. *Maybe his contrary streak is finally playing itself out,* Alec thought.

One night, Alec entered the training barn and found Creo halfway down the corridor, cleaning tack in front of Storm's stall. The colt was bobbing his head over the stall door, in tune to a soft, rhythmic chanting sound. Creo was half rapping, half singing to the colt as his fingers worked the leather. He seemed completely focused on Storm, and the colt was equally focused on him.

Suddenly, Creo realized someone was coming. He froze for a moment, then relaxed when he saw it was only Alec. A grin dimpled his cheeks and made his eyes crinkle slightly at the corners. "Alec, my man." He put his hand out, palm up. Alec slapped it once, gently.

"Storm's in a mellow mood tonight," Alec said.

Creo returned his gaze to the colt. "He's a good boy, aren't you, guy?"

Alec smiled. "I guess he can be when he wants to be. Last week...forget about it! One morning he almost kicked his stall door in." Alec rolled his eyes.

Creo nodded. "Yeah, I saw the hoof marks." He picked up another bridle as Alec sat down on the bench beside him.

"Is Henry treating you okay?" Alec asked.

"He's keeping me busy," Creo answered with a shrug.

"The guy's not flashy like some of the trainers you might see at the track," Alec said. "But he's saddled as many winners as any of those guys."

"Old school, like you say."

The two of them fell quiet for a few moments. It was a comfortable silence, the sort that comes at the end of a long, hard day. Storm neighed softly. Then the fine, delicately sculpted head drew back into the shadows of the stall.

Alec sighed. "I swear Henry's wrong about that horse, though."

Creo nodded. "I'm with you on that. You know,

when I first found Storm back in Brooklyn, I almost thought it was some kind of miracle. I just couldn't accept the idea that he might belong to someone else. I guess I even thought he'd been sent to me, somehow. It was the first thing I'd ever wanted that was really going to be all mine. Does that sound stupid?"

"Not at all," Alec said. "I felt the same way the first time I saw the Black."

Creo sighed. "At least Storm and I are together again."

"There you go," Alec said. "That's great."

They were silent again for a while, each lost in thought. Alec always enjoyed listening to the peaceful night sounds of the barn. Finally, he said, "Look, Creo. It's pretty obvious you want to get up on Storm again. And I think—maybe, just maybe—once Henry sees you ride, he won't object. I'll have a talk with him about it. You're caught up on your chores. You've earned a ride, I think."

Creo was clearly trying not to sound too anxious, but Alec could tell he was excited. "I'm ready anytime you say."

"Remember, Henry might not go for this," Alec warned. He didn't want the kid to be disappointed. "He's real particular about who he puts up on his charges."

"He'll let me. I know he will. And, uh, Alec"—Creo hesitated—"I mean, well, I...just wanted to thank you again for everything. For the job and everything. I really—"

"That was Henry's decision," Alec broke in. "He could tell you knew what you were doing."

"Well, thanks anyway." Creo looked down at the floor.

"Why don't you take a break?" Alec said. "Get some sleep. You've cleaned enough leather for one day."

Creo picked up a bridle. "I'm almost finished."

Alec stood up. "Well, I need to look over some paperwork in the office. It never seems to end. See you in the morning, okay?"

Creo nodded. "Good night."

As Alec walked back down the corridor, he heard Creo start chanting his rap for Storm again, making popping noises with his mouth like a drum machine. The tone was reassuring, the punching rhythm soft and hypnotic. Alec glanced over his shoulder and saw that the colt's head was bobbing over the stall door once again. He smiled. Could this be the same colt who had nearly kicked in his stall door the other day? There was no doubt that the kid from Brooklyn had a calming effect on Storm.

Later that night, as Alec lay in bed, he thought of what Creo had said about seeing Storm for the first time. His mind drifted back to a time four years earlier, to the small Arabian port town where he'd first spotted the Black. He remembered the shipwreck and the deserted island to which the Black had carried him. He imagined he was there once again, riding the Black alone on the beach. Sun, sea, and sky. Water splashing his thighs. Everything seemed so clear, so real. Alec could taste the salty sea air, feel the wind, hear hoofs cantering across hard, wet sand. Before long, the dream lulled him into a deep sleep.

CHAPTER EIGHT

A Surprise Visitor

Alec left the house for work at five-thirty the next morning, still feeling sleepy and running a little late. When he stepped outside, only a faint trace of purple light colored the eastern horizon. The air felt cool and wet. He blew on his cold hands and stuffed them into the pockets of his denim jacket.

Inside the training barn, Creo and Deb were already busy moving from stall to stall. They were mucking out soiled straw and feeding and grooming each horse in turn. Henry sat on a bench outside the tack room, thumbing through some notes on his clipboard.

Barely a word passed among them. Together they were a team. Each person knew his job and set about doing it with a minimum of fuss or talk.

Alec saddled his first mount of the day, Black Wind. After checking the tension on the girth strap, he unclipped the filly from the crossties and walked her outside.

For the next few hours, Alec exercised the horses stabled in the training barn, putting them through their custom-tailored regimes. After each ride, he returned to the daybook chart posted on the wall of the tack room and methodically penciled in his comments. Storm's name languished at the bottom of the list, under the heading "Optional."

Halfway through the list, Alec glanced at the next slot in the morning's program and did a double take. "What's this?" he muttered under his breath. He had already exercised Black Tower this morning, and the colt was marked down again for the ten o'clock slot. That couldn't be right. Henry must have made a mistake when he updated the chart. Alec shook his head. Sometimes he thought the old trainer was losing it.

He looked around the barn for Henry to tell him about the mix-up, but he saw no sign of the trainer. Deb was walking Black Aces around the barn, twirling the end of the lead rope in his hand. Alec caught up to them.

"Hey, Deb!" Alec called. "Seen Henry around?"

The groom looked over his shoulder. "Nope," he

said, yawning. "Any doughnuts left in the kitchen?"

Alec shook his head and gave Aces a pat on the neck. They walked together around the side of the barn, and Deb pointed toward the driveway. "Henry's truck is gone," he said.

"He must have gone to town for something," Alec said.

"Well, I hope he brings us back something to eat," Deb said. "I'm starving." Aces reached over and tried to take a nip out of his shoulder. The groom flinched just in time and then lightly smacked the colt on the muzzle with the end of the lead rope.

He chuckled. "Looks like everybody's getting hungry around here."

Alec walked back inside the barn and went to check the daybook again, moving his finger across the column of names.

Wait a minute! he thought suddenly. Maybe he could use the hole in the training schedule to give Storm a short workout. Nothing serious, he told himself, just something to open up the colt's windpipe a bit. Storm was in the "Optional" group, after all. And something told him he'd better take advantage of the opportunity. It might be his only chance for a long while to give Storm a workout.

Alec brought the black colt out of the barn. Storm looked terrific, his powerful muscles sculpted in fine curves and his coat gleaming like wild silk in the morning sun. The colt bounced around impatiently, jigging on his toes, his tail swaying dramatically. Alec gave him a pat on the neck and tried to scratch the colt behind his ears. Storm jerked his head away.

"Ease up, Storm," Alec said, annoyed. "Why do you have to be this way?" The colt gave a half rear and danced back restlessly. Alec moved with him, trying to be patient.

After a few more antics, Storm finally stood still enough for Alec to mount him. All the way to the training track, Alec sang to the colt, making up the lyrics as he rode along. *It worked for Creo,* he told himself.

For a few moments, Storm's mood settled, then became sullen and dark. "Talk about temperamental," Alec muttered, bracing himself for the colt's next move.

But the colt perked up again once they reached the track. Alec put him into motion, shifting his weight forward. Storm responded gamely when Alec broke him into a gallop. The colt took a firm hold on the bit, and Alec didn't try to stop him.

After one circuit of the training track, the colt moved into overdrive. *So much for the light pipe opener,* Alec thought. By now, Storm was practically pulling Alec's arms out. Through two entire circuits, all Alec could do was keep his balance and steer.

Finally, Alec managed to pull up the colt. He gave Storm an affectionate slap on the neck. "Atta boy-ee, atta boy-ee," he whispered, sinking the heels of his boots back into the stirrups. Slowly, he leaned farther back and stood up in his irons. Storm was snorting like a slowing locomotive.

Alec glanced at his watch. There was still time left, and no question that Storm still had plenty of gas left in the tank. Alec's attention shifted to the barn. No sign of Henry, either. Good. He had a pretty fair guess as to how the old trainer would feel if he saw Alec taking Storm over any jumps.

After setting up four hurdles at furlong intervals, Alec was astride Storm again, looking down the stretch to the first jump. He took a deep breath, trying to reinforce his confidence in Storm. He knew he had to be careful. He had never known a horse with a split personality like this. He couldn't take any chances on an accident now, nothing that would further complicate the colt's education—or jeopardize his own health. Alec changed his grip on the reins and gave a nudge with his heels. Once again, Storm was off and running.

The colt cleared the first two hedges, tucking his knees up to his chin and sailing over with inches to spare. He was gaining ground with every stride, sprinting on to meet the next challenge. After the bend and the next jump, he picked up even more speed. Alec edged him closer to the inside rail.

The wind whistling by Alec's ears changed pitch slightly. It was a barely perceptible change, a subtle imbalance. Alec knew he was riding a double handful of horse, but he started to feel as if something was off. The faint tick became a twitch, but it wasn't defined enough to make Alec shift his weight.

Charging on toward the final jump, the rhythm of Storm's pounding hoofs suddenly broke completely. Alec tried to keep Storm together with legs and hands, but he quickly realized he was making a serious mistake. The colt crashed headlong into the hurdle.

Alec lost his stirrups and dove through the air. Keeping himself loose, he tucked his legs beneath him, knees to his stomach, his head protected under his arms. He somersaulted over and over through the air, then hit the ground hard, rolling in the grass.

Moments passed. As soon as his vision cleared, Alec raised the upper part of his body. With a groan, he stiffly began pulling himself to his feet. He took off his helmet to rub his head and tried to collect himself. Slowly, the buzzing numbness began to drain from his body.

Another spill, Alec thought, sighing. This was getting to be a painful routine. Storm paced back and forth a few yards away, acting as if nothing had happened. Thanks to the forgiving nature of the brush fence, the colt seemed to have come through the ordeal without injuring himself. His nostrils flared as he sniffed the air, his eyes quivering. He swung his head toward Alec, undecided, uneasy. He continued to paw the ground, snorting with impatience.

Alec took the reins and started to walk the colt back toward the barn. It was then that he caught sight of the slightly mud-spattered white Cadillac and the figure leaning against the fence rail. When the man lowered the binoculars from his face, Alec recognized him: Luke Stedman. *What is he doing here?* Alec wondered. He wasn't supposed to come by the farm until tomorrow!

The man stubbed out his cigar. Then he slipped through the fence railing and swaggered out to meet Alec.

Alec felt a bit nervous about this surprise visit. Who wouldn't be? Right now, Luke Stedman was rated as one of the top trainers in the country. It hardly mattered that neither Alec nor Henry thought much of Stedman personally—the man was notorious for being aggressive and brash. But trainers in Stedman's league could afford to be unpopular. All that mattered to the owners was that he brought home winners.

Stedman had close-cropped white hair, the cold blue eyes of a professional gambler, and a deep, almost coffee-colored suntan. He was wearing a white short-sleeve shirt and starched jeans. A gold medallion on a thick chain showed at his throat, and designer sunglasses hung against his chest on a cord.

Stedman gave Alec a big-toothed smile, prominent canines gleaming at the corners of his mouth. "That was some tumble, kid," he said. "You all right?"

"I fell in the right way. Lucky, I guess," Alec said, shrugging. He wiped a spot of grime from his forehead with his shirt sleeve.

"The colt was looking pretty good there." Stedman smiled again, his lips pulling away from his teeth with no hint of warmth or humor. "He the one you had the reward out for?"

Alec nodded. "Yup."

"Thought so. Heard about that spill you two took out over at Belmont. Too bad. Looks like somebody's trying to tell you something, kid." Stedman did his best to appear concerned. Alec did his best to keep a smile on his face. They shook hands.

Alec made courteous small talk, something that felt painfully embarrassing under the circumstances.

This wasn't just a matter of being polite, he reminded himself. People like Luke Stedman were essential to the livelihood of Hopeful Farm. This was a bottom-line business. Hopeful Farm needed customers, and Black Orchid and Jet Set were for sale. With any luck, Stedman might make them a decent offer.

Finally, Alec nodded toward the barn. "Henry's probably in the office. I'd better get Jet Set tacked up." He hoisted himself back into the saddle.

Stedman watched them canter off, his cool eyes clearly appraising Storm's every move. A faint smile crept across his lips. Then he walked back to his Cadillac, got inside, and slowly drove up the rest of the driveway to the Hopeful Farm office.

CHAPTER NINE

A Bad Bargain

Back at the training barn, Alec dismounted and turned Storm over to Deb. Creo was sweeping out the corridor between the stalls. He stared after Storm longingly as Deb led the colt away. "I didn't know you were exercising him today. How'd he run for you?" Creo asked.

"I'll tell you about it later, okay?" Alec said. Creo raised his eyebrows, but he nodded and went back to work.

Luke Stedman walked up from where he'd parked his car. Once again his critical gaze followed Storm. Creo watched him suspiciously as he eyed the colt.

Alec escorted Stedman inside the barn. They picked their way to the office past saddles, blankets, pitchforks, wheelbarrows, and old copies of the *Daily Racing Form*. The office door was open and Henry was at his desk, talking on the phone. When he saw Stedman, he sat up and gestured at the chair in front of his desk. Stedman nodded and sat down. Curious to find out what Stedman was up to, Alec went over and began to sort through some mail on his desk as an excuse to hang around.

"All right, Jerry," Henry quickly finished up. "Two o'clock. Yes. Talk to you soon." He hung up the phone and leaned forward, glancing at Alec and then back at Stedman. "Mr. Luke," he said, raising one eyebrow. "Well, what do you know. We didn't expect you until tomorrow." Henry hated surprise visitors, Alec knew. There was something testy beneath his welcoming words.

Henry stood and put out his hand as a professional courtesy. Stedman half rose to take it, and they both sat down again.

"I should have called first, I know," Stedman said, "but I was in the area and thought I'd drop by. If you want me to come back later..." He turned up the palms of his hands and shrugged as if to apologize.

"No, no," Henry assured him quickly. "We're always glad to see you, Luke. Let me get the latest printouts on those two fillies we spoke about."

"If it's not too much trouble."

This guy is so phony, Alec told himself. And it bothered him a bit to see Henry having to butter up someone like Stedman. But that was life—or business anyway.

Henry reached over to the computer on the table beside his desk and flipped it on. When the screen brightened, he tapped a few keys and a list of names appeared. He highlighted the files for Jet Set and Black Orchid and punched the keyboard again. The printer came to life and quickly spit out the vital statistics on the two fillies.

Henry gave Alec a quick up-and-down glance, noting the streaks of mud smearing Alec's jacket and jeans. "What happened to you?"

"Oh, nothing." *Here it comes,* thought Alec. *Please let's not get into this now!*

"Yeah?" asked Henry, watching Alec and waiting.

"Your boy took a little spill," Stedman chimed in cheerfully. "Saw it on my way here. I was kind of worried about him for a minute there. But he's a tough kid." Stedman gave Alec a big man-to-man smile. "Aren't you, sport?"

Alec tried to smile back through clenched teeth.

"Little spill, huh?" Henry asked expectantly.

"Storm balked at one of the hurdles on the turf course. Dumped me. He's okay."

Henry suddenly seemed to forget that Stedman was in the room at all. His voice was steely quiet, but he couldn't conceal his disgust. "Hurdles?" His eyes flashed angrily. "What the heck were you doing, Alec? Sitting on your brains? You're not even supposed to be working with Storm today."

"It was nothing," Alec said. "Let's talk about this later, okay?"

Shaking his head, Henry turned to Stedman. "Want to buy a horse, Luke?" he asked. "Cheap. Maybe you'd have better luck with that colt than I've had."

"You mean that colt I just saw?" Stedman said, pretending to be surprised. "What'd you say his name was again? Cyclone or something?"

Spare me, you phony, Alec thought. *As if you don't know.*

"Storm," Henry said, playing along. "Black Storm."

"He's a pretty animal."

"Five grand and he's yours."

Alec blinked. *What?* Was this some sort of joke? Henry couldn't be serious! "Wait a minute, Henry," Alec broke in. "Don't you think we'd better…"

Henry cut off Alec's words with a cold, hard stare.

Stedman ran his hand across his forehead and patted his hair, seeming to enjoy watching the squabble sparking up between Alec and Henry. A little smile crept across his lips. "I'll keep it in mind, Henry."

Henry picked up his fedora and stepped around the desk. "In the meantime, let's take a look at those fillies. Alec, get to work, will you? Mr. Stedman here is a busy man." He put his arm around Stedman's shoulder and guided him through the door.

Alec followed after them and almost bumped into Creo, who was sweeping up outside the office door. By the look on the young groom's face, Alec could tell that Creo must have heard some of what Henry had said about Storm. Creo watched the man warily as he passed. "Come on, Creo," Alec said. "You can give me a hand getting Jet Set and Black Orchid tacked up."

Creo gave a nod. As Stedman walked ahead, discussing one of his horses with Henry, Creo turned to Alec. "Henry wasn't serious, was he? He's not really selling Storm to that guy, right?"

"I don't know, Creo," Alec said, still finding it hard himself to believe what he'd just heard. Sure, Storm was for sale. But they couldn't just give the colt away. *Five grand.* Some of the people Stedman represented had that kind of money in their change jars.

Henry and Stedman waited for them over at the training track. Alec tried to force all thoughts of Storm from his mind and concentrate on the job at hand. After they'd finished tacking Jet Set, Alec unclipped the filly from the crossties and led her outside.

The gray filly was a big, strong girl, a good sixteen hands, with deep shoulders and chest and a muscular, arched neck. If she had a problem, it was one of being too eager, running too fast at the start of a workout and too slow at the end.

Behind them, Creo was walking Black Orchid, a lightly framed dark bay, with a long, thick mane. She was as beautiful and delicate a filly as her name implied. But Orchid could be a bit too easygoing, almost to the point of laziness.

The conditions of both the fillies were ones that horsemen and -women confronted practically every day on the training track. There were different schools of thought on how to handle them, but they were far from unusual. Compared to Storm's, their problems were simple.

A few minutes later, Alec was mounted up and ready to go. He guided Jet Set through the gap in the training track gate and, at a signal from Henry, put her in motion. She fired into a sprint for the first two furlongs but slacked off for the last two, despite all of Alec's urgings.

When it was Black Orchid's turn, the filly rolled into a gallop with long, easy strides. For once, she was all business as Alec asked her to breeze a furlong. After two circuits of the training track, Henry gave Alec the wrap-it-up signal. Alec walked Orchid to the barn and turned her over to Creo.

Despite the mediocre workouts, Alec, Henry, and especially Luke Stedman knew that, at this point in their young careers, the two fillies' true potential had merely been scratched. Their breeding suggested inexhaustible strength, endurance, and spirit. With any luck, after being put through a custom-tailored training regime, both would develop into horses to be reckoned with on the racetrack.

When Alec joined Henry and Stedman at rail side, the Floridian was giving his polite approval of the fillies. "Fine animals, those two. Especially that Black Orchid."

Alec tried to read the sincerity of the expression on Stedman's face. Henry looked tense. Both men were locked into serious horse-trading mode. Finally, Stedman said he had to get off to another appointment and thanked Alec and Henry for their time.

A Bad Bargain

After he left, Alec turned to Henry. "So how'd it go? Is he buying or just looking?"

Henry stared off in the direction of the training track. "Looking, I think."

There was a moment of brooding silence. *Here it comes,* Alec thought. *Better launch a preemptive strike.* Before Henry could say anything, Alec started to explain about the hole in the training schedule, about how well Storm had been running, and about how the fall was his own mistake.

Henry bowled right over him. "Alec, are you out of your mind? What were you trying to do?" He ranted on for a while, then wound down into grumbling about Storm. "Maybe we'll get lucky, and Stedman will take that colt off our hands for real," he said.

Alec's temper flared. "For that kind of money, who wouldn't want him? That's less than half what we should get for *any* horse on the farm!"

Henry lowered his voice. It sounded hard but not unkind, all matter-of-fact, all business. "You know the situation, Alec. The farm needs money and plenty of it. Right now."

"What does that have to do with practically giving Storm away?"

"The colt's unmanageable. A liability. If you keep trying to put him over hurdles, you're going to

97

get hurt. And that's not just your problem. Anything that happens to you affects Hopeful Farm. That makes it *my* problem, too."

Alec took a deep breath to calm his nerves. "It was nothing, Henry. My fault, really. If you could just..."

Henry held up his hand for Alec to stop, as if the matter had already been decided. "Sorry, Alec. The first chance we get, Storm's outta here. History. We're cutting our losses and moving on. At this point, five grand will just about pay his feed bill and a bit of the time we've put into him so far." He gave Alec a skeptical shake of his head and turned around to walk back to the office. Alec stood there for a moment, still feeling the sting of Henry's words. Somewhere inside of him, a voice said, *"Take it easy. Henry's just talking. Storm's not going anywhere."*

Another voice countered, *"Right. When word gets out that a colt sired by the Black is selling for that kind of money, he'll be lucky to last the week here."*

Alec kicked the dirt in frustration. If only he hadn't tried to take Storm over the hurdles this morning. He played the ride over again once more in his mind, trying to analyze it down to the last hurdle, the little tick that threw Storm off his stride.

Maybe he was thinking about this whole thing

too much. What he really needed was to step back, to watch Storm from a different perspective. For that, though, he'd need another rider. Creo could do it, no doubt. Unfortunately, in Henry's present state of mind, Storm would be lucky to get out of the barn again by next week. Also, the chances of the old trainer's letting Creo saddle one of the horses were virtually nil.

Alec rubbed his chin. On the other hand, Henry was going to town tomorrow afternoon. Maybe he wouldn't even need to know about it.

CHAPTER TEN

Racing Against the Clock

As soon as Henry left for his meeting in town the next afternoon, Alec moved into action. He pushed away the pile of bills he'd been wading through and strode down the barn corridor to Storm's stall.

There must be something I can do to get through to that horse, Alec thought. But how much time did he have before Stedman or someone like him bought Storm? And was schooling the colt really worth the risk of making Henry even angrier? Alec's jaw clenched in frustration. This whole thing made him feel so confused.

The barn was quiet except for the drone of Deb's gentle voice. The old groom was brushing one of

Hopeful Farm's rising young stars, the leggy bay colt named Black Aces.

"That's my boy, Aces. Only three days left till the big day. Oh, you're sure gonna like Saratoga, with all those pretty fillies running around. But you keep your mind on business, you hear? I will personally kick your butt all the way to Jersey if you don't win. I've been saving up all month for a bet on that race." Deb stressed the point with a grunt. "Umph. Man, you are a big, beautiful monster! You can't lose." Aces concentrated on his supper.

On the other side of the barn, Creo was raking up loose clumps of dirty straw and pitchforking them into a wheelbarrow. He glanced up at Alec and nodded a greeting. Alec signaled to Creo with a wave, nodding his head toward Storm's stall.

Creo looked puzzled. Alec signaled again. A conspiratorial smile edged across Creo's face. He finally seemed to have gotten the message. This was it, his chance to ride Storm again. "Let's go, Creo," Alec said quietly. "It's time."

Alec found an extra riding helmet and a pair of boots in the tack closet. Creo quickly finished what he was doing, pulled off his sneakers, and slid his feet into the boots. Then they tacked up Storm and brought him out of the barn.

Alec ran his hand down Storm's shoulder and his front legs, patting him in a confident, satisfied way. Despite the knocks the colt had taken yesterday, he looked fit, tight, and full of power.

Deb appeared at the barn entrance and shook his head warily. "You just don't quit, do you?" he called to Alec.

Alec fumbled with the cinch on Storm's saddle. "Not if I think I'm right."

"Sure, you're a little bulldog, you are. What's Henry going to say about you messin' around with Storm again?"

"I don't know, Deb."

The old groom looked worried. Then he gave a weary, seen-it-all-before shrug. "You've always been a kid who had to live and learn." He glanced over at Creo. "But be careful with our young friend here. We're just gettin' him broken in. Don't go killing him off just yet. Good barn help's too hard to come by." He winked.

"Wouldn't think of it, Deb," Alec said with a grin. "He's taking a couple turns around the turf course, that's all."

Creo beamed. "I can handle Storm, Alec. You know that."

With a quick hop-step-jump, Creo vaulted onto

Storm's back, barely touching the stirrups. Storm jigged around a moment, then grew still. Creo leaned forward to whisper something low and soft to the colt—soothing words, as if he was letting him in on a very personal secret.

"Ride out to the gap and wait for me there," Alec told Creo. Then he left to get the Black.

Out on the turf course, Storm and the Black eyed each other warily. Their ears pricked forward, then lay back, and their thin-skinned nostrils quivered. Storm's small head kept nodding and poking, his long legs shifting cautiously in the grass.

The Black was always intimidating to other horses and riders, but Creo did his best to seem unfazed about having the legendary champion for a pacesetter. But as cool as he tried to act, Creo had to know his first ride at Hopeful Farm was one of the most important moments in his life. The pressure was on.

Alec smiled. "Just let Storm follow the Black's lead, okay?"

"Sure."

"How does he seem to you?"

"Great."

"Okay, then. Let's do it."

Creo gave a short nod and put Storm into

motion. As the colt took off, Alec called, "Let him stride out the last couple of furlongs, but don't go crazy! Hear me, Creo? Creo!"

But Creo was already lost in a dipping canter, straddling high and stiff-legged, his mind and body completely focused on Storm. Alec squeezed his heels and hurried the Black after them.

Like the Black, Storm had a long, easy stride. At a gallop, Creo started coming down to his seat, smooth and slow. Storm's rocking never reached his body.

Creo crouched forward on the colt's neck. Alec changed his grip on the reins and followed suit. The Black moved effortlessly into cruising speed, his black mane flowing behind him like wind-swept flame.

The two horses accelerated smoothly around the far turn with neither jockey appearing to lean or move a muscle. Storm was still running in front. Then the Black started to move. He and Alec were connected like a firm handshake, a single entity for which nothing existed save the next few feet of track. Alec let the reins out another notch, and the Black shot by the colt like a train, the stallion taking one stride for every two of Storm's.

Alec eased back in his seat and let Storm catch up. The horses turned in together and came up the straight stride for stride. Creo glanced over and said something Alec couldn't understand. He saw the kid tighten his crouch, gluing himself flat to Storm's neck.

Storm began to move again, stretching legs and neck. Alec kept a tight hold on the reins and let them pass. By the time they crossed the mile marker a second time and pulled up, Creo had Storm three lengths in the clear.

The expression on Creo's face was ecstatic. Alec waved. "Not bad!" he called.

"This horse is on fire, boss," Creo called back, breathless from the ride. He slid his hand down and slapped Storm's neck softly. The breathing of both horses came in big heaves as they walked up the straight, side by side.

"Did Storm feel a little anxious to you," Alec asked, "going into that last turn?"

Creo pulled his racing goggles up onto his helmet. "Not really anxious," he said. "More like eager. Too eager."

Alec nodded in agreement. "Yeah. Like he doesn't know his own strength."

Storm nickered softly. For the moment, the colt seemed as friendly and well behaved as anyone could ask. This time it was the Black's turn to start acting up. The stallion gave a loud snort, threatening to swing his hindquarters toward Storm.

"Ho!" Alec called. The Black whinnied a piercing challenge to Storm, just to make sure the colt knew who was in charge.

Storm heard the challenge and gave a push back, half rearing on his long hind legs. With a warning snap of the reins, Creo leaned forward, trying to keep Storm's forelegs on the ground.

"That's enough nonsense from you two," Alec said sharply, then turned to Creo. "Take Storm on ahead, okay?"

Creo reined Storm around. "See ya," he called over his shoulder.

Alec nudged the Black ahead. They took the long way home, following the path along the upper pasture.

With his ears pricked forward, the Black watched Storm prancing off to the barn. "Troublemaker," Alec scolded him.

Well, he told himself, he'd gotten his chance to watch Storm from a different vantage point. But what had he really learned? That on a good day Storm loved to run? He knew that already. That Storm was overeager? Well, yes, but that was good—the colt needed that will to win.

No, Alec told himself. The trouble with Storm was consistency. And he still felt at a loss for an explanation.

A fresh breeze swept down upon him, and Alec found he was listening, as if he might hear a voice on the wind—the kind of calm and reassuring voice that made everything clear, that whispered, "Have you thought of this?" But Alec didn't hear any voice, and he knew he wasn't going to. Nobody was going to explain this one to him. He'd have to figure it out on his own.

CHAPTER ELEVEN

Last Chance

Alec turned the Black out in the far pasture, then headed back to the barn to check the schedule for the rest of the afternoon. Henry came back from town and set to work halter-breaking the yearlings. Creo was busy cleaning feed tubs. Deb rolled bandages. No one said a word about Storm.

At the end of the day, after working the last horse on the afternoon program, Alec walked wearily into the office.

Fishing out a recent copy of *Turf Reporter* from the stack of horse racing magazines on a shelf beside the door, he sat down at his desk and cleared a space for himself by pushing away the pile of bills stacked in front of him.

Alec fanned through the pages and stopped at a photograph of a pair of steeplechasers in mid-flight. *There it is,* he thought. He knew he hadn't imagined seeing that notice. He read it again and smiled. This could be just the opportunity he'd been waiting for— a chance for Storm to prove himself.

The glossy, full-page ad announced the upcoming Pennsylvania Gold Cup, a two-mile-long hurdle race. The major corporate sponsors were donating a thirty-thousand-dollar purse for the winner. That was decent money for a regional steeplechase. Alec folded back the page and rushed out of the office to find Henry.

The trainer was standing outside the paddock, where he'd just turned out the last two yearlings. The frisky colts were bucking and playing, chasing each other in the warm afternoon sun. Henry looked a little surprised to see Alec. "Everything okay?"

"Just fine." Alec handed Henry the magazine. "I thought you should take a look at this."

Henry glanced at the ad and shrugged. "So?"

"I know we usually don't go in for these sort of deals, but for thirty grand I thought maybe..."

"You want to sign up for this thing?" Henry said incredulously.

Alec nodded.

Henry pushed the magazine back into Alec's

hand. "And let me guess which horse you want to ride."

"He's doing a lot better, Henry. Really, he is. And if we're lucky, there's still time to nominate Storm for the Gold Cup. It'd be a perfect trial race for him."

"Trial race? What did you call the other day at Belmont? It seems to me he's had one trial race already and you ended up with your face in the dirt."

"Come on, Henry. Think of all we'd gain if Storm did well. If not, we couldn't be any worse off than we are right now."

Henry shook his head, looking serious. "We don't have any business running jumpers. It's not my style, and it's not yours either. How many times do I have to…"

"Please, Henry, give me and Storm a chance. You can't make a decision just like that."

"Is that so, huh?"

"Thirty thousand dollars, Henry. Don't you think it's at least worth a shot?"

Henry pushed his beat-up fedora back on his head and sighed. The expression on his face was part amazement, part aggravation, and part disgust.

"Please, Henry," Alec said again. "Just one more chance, that's all I'm asking."

"All this nonsense is driving me nuts," Henry

said. "But if it means that much to you, kid...okay, we'll enter the colt in the Cup. Take a few days and we'll look at your times. It'll be worth it just to have you stop badgering me about this whole thing. But we scratch the colt if he doesn't show us something. Is that fair enough?"

Alec breathed a sigh of relief. "You won't regret this, Henry. I promise."

Henry just grunted and walked away.

When Alec told Creo that he was entering Storm in the Gold Cup, the groom's mouth fell open with shock. "You mean it?"

"Yup. So we're going to be rearranging the schedule around here a bit. We'll be getting up even earlier and working later."

"Whatever you say!" Creo said excitedly.

"It also means I'm going to need you to ride with us regularly as a pacesetter. I'm sure Henry will agree, as long as you're caught up with the rest of your chores. Think you can handle that?"

Creo smiled. "Try and stop me."

For the next few days, Alec worked Storm in the afternoons after exercising all the other horses in the training barn. He hardly missed the lost hours of sleep, figuring it was a small price to pay to give Storm his shot.

During their workouts together, Creo usually

rode Black Orbit or one of the other more docile horses. As thrilled as the kid seemed to be riding a sleek thoroughbred like Orbit knee-to-knee with an experienced jockey, Alec could tell Creo was a little jealous of Alec getting to ride Storm. But this was serious business. Alec had to get Storm—and himself—in the best possible shape for the Gold Cup.

Once or twice, though, Alec did let Creo have the ride on Storm while Alec used the Black as a pacesetter. During those workouts, Alec and the Black *really* gave Storm something to run at. The colt had little choice, unless he wanted to be left in the dust. It was a little embarrassing for Alec, but hardly surprising, that Storm turned in his best times with Creo in the saddle, running against the Black.

Creo's excitement couldn't help but feed Alec's own enthusiasm. And the more time the two of them spent together, the more Alec began to think of Creo as a pal rather than an employee. As they discussed Storm, the Black, the other horses at Hopeful Farm, and the qualities of some of the top jockeys they both admired, a mutual respect and friendship grew between them.

Steadily, Storm's workouts began to improve— or at least Alec thought so. The colt took to the jumps with natural balletic leaps. His giant strides ate up the distance between the fences. His stable manners also seemed to improve with no bucking or shying. Storm was becoming almost dependable.

But Henry wasn't easy to impress. He rarely intervened in Storm's workouts, either, except to offer an occasional brief compliment or criticism. No news was good news with Henry. He'd followed through with his promise to nominate Storm for the Cup race. And so far, there were no threats of scratching Storm from the Gold Cup.

The trainer waved him over as Alec pulled up Storm after their latest workout. He glowered at his stopwatch, holding it up for Alec to see. Alec sighed. Henry had been in a cranky mood all day.

He nodded, trying to be optimistic. "Not bad. A second and a half better than before that race at Belmont."

"Well, that isn't saying much," Henry said. "And Storm ain't going to be running against the clock in the Gold Cup. You two are going to be out there with a card full of seasoned hurdle jocks, saddling veteran steeplechasers. They're gonna be out for blood. They'll kill you."

"What about Storm's time yesterday with Creo?" Alec pointed out. "They cut a full second off my best time for the mile."

"The way that kid rides, we're just lucky he didn't fall off and sue us," Henry said. Alec hid a smile. The truth was, if Henry really didn't like the way Creo rode, he would never have let him saddle one of the Hopeful Farm horses, even Storm.

Henry shook his head. "What that colt wants to do on Wednesday, he won't do on Thursday. Then on Friday he won't do what he wanted to do so badly on Wednesday. That animal just wants to be left alone."

"He's too smart for his own good, that's all," Alec argued. "He has to be kept interested in the race. We're really starting to get something out of him now. We just can't push him too hard, that's all."

"*Push* him?" Henry burst out. "He's not giving us anything to push. And the Cup race is in one week!"

CHAPTER TWELVE

One-Way Ticket

Despite Henry's eternal pessimism, Storm continued to behave himself over the next few days, gradually shaving fractions off his time around the hurdle course. Alec felt sure that the patience and understanding that he and Creo had shown the colt were finally paying off.

One night, Alec's parents called from California to check in. Alec assured them that everything was fine. They were relieved to hear that Henry had fully recovered from the attack and supportive when Alec told them about Storm. Of the two of them, Alec's mom was generally the bigger worrier, but she agreed with Alec's dad that Alec had proved he was mature enough to be making his own decisions. Then Henry got on the phone and assured Mr. and Mrs. Ramsay that things were under control. Alec breathed a sigh of relief as he hung up.

On Tuesday afternoon, three days before the race, Creo brought Storm into the barn. He had just finished washing and cooling out the colt. Storm's coat shone like dark velvet under his exercise sheet as Creo walked him down the corridor to his stall. Creo gave a mock salute as the two of them passed Henry, who was hanging a bridle on a tack rack that was overloaded with riding gear.

Suddenly, there was a loud *crack* and a hundred pounds of tack cascaded to the barn floor. Henry jumped out of the way just in time, sprawling on his backside.

The sound of the crash behind him threw Storm into a panic. He reared up, jerking the reins out of Creo's hands and shying violently. The colt bolted down the corridor, his eyes bulging with wild fear, his ears flat against the top of his head. Only one thing stood in his way at the other end of the barn: Alec.

Alec's first thought was for Storm. He had to stop the colt from hurting himself in his wild charge through the barn. Almost instinctively, Alec planted his legs and waved his arms. Storm's shrill scream cracked like thunder through the barn. Panic had turned to blind fury. The colt wasn't going to stop!

Alec had no time left to think. Storm was upon

him, mouth open, teeth gleaming, eyes blazing with mad rage.

At the last second, Alec jumped away. He landed in a heap, crumpled up against the office door. Storm thundered past, bursting out of the barn and into the sunlight.

"Alec!" Henry cried, running toward him. Creo was close behind.

Alec raised a hand. "I'm okay," he said shakily.

Henry whirled around and glared at Creo. "Well, what are *you* standing around for?" he sputtered. "Get after that crazy animal! *Go!*"

For a moment, Creo looked stunned. Then he sprinted after Storm, who was hightailing it up the driveway. Henry helped Alec to his feet and jerked his thumb after Creo. "What's with that kid, anyway?"

"It was an accident, Henry," Alec said wearily. "Besides, *you* were the one who busted the tack loose."

"That's because the rack was overloaded to start with," Henry grumbled. "Are you sure you're okay?"

"I'm fine, Henry," Alec said, limping over to the truck. "Maybe I can cut Storm off before he reaches the road."

"Let Creo go after the colt," Henry called after him. "We have work to do. Come on."

In the distance, Alec heard Creo calling to the colt. A hint of desperation sounded in his cries. *Everything had been going so well,* Alec thought miserably. *And now this had to happen.* He sighed and followed Henry back into the barn.

That night Henry called Alec into the office and closed the door. There was no light except the glow from the green-shaded banker's lamp on the trainer's desk. Behind the desk, Henry sat in the shadows, looking bleary-eyed and haggard. The mood in the dark room made Alec feel uneasy.

"What's up?" Alec asked.

Henry folded his thick arms across his chest and tilted his chair back. "Guess who I spoke to today? Pete Hartman. He's looking for a job."

Alec conjured up a picture of Pete, a forty-something retired jockey. They'd been trying to get Pete to come work at Hopeful Farm for years. Aside from being a terrific rider, he was an experienced and dependable hand in the foaling barn.

"I thought we might take him on."

Alec nodded. "Sounds great."

"Of course, we'll have to cut Creo loose."

Alec blinked. "What do you mean? He's been doing great. You're not still blaming him for what happened with Storm today, are you?"

Henry looked away. "The kid knew his position was only temporary when he hired on," he said. "Temporary, Alec, as in *not permanent*. It was just supposed to be until we could find professional help, remember? Well, Pete's about as qualified as a person can be."

This isn't right! Alec thought. "Give the kid a break, Henry," he pleaded. "You know he'd work for practically nothing just to stay."

"Get serious, will you, Alec? This isn't some charity summer camp," Henry said sharply. "Besides, Creo will never wear silks. He hasn't the balance, the judgment, or the brains to ride competitively. And he is already as big as you are."

"Okay, so he's big," Alec argued. "But the rest of that just isn't true. You've seen him ride. He's got talent, over the jumps and on the flats. He can even handle Storm."

Henry didn't answer. He looked away and began to turn his attention to some papers on his desk. Alec could tell that nothing he said was going to change the old trainer's mind. "Okay, I'll go tell him," Alec said finally. Maybe he could at least stall for time.

But Henry wasn't to be put off so easily.

"I already did," he said, without looking up.

Alec stared at Henry. *Don't you know what this will do to Creo?* he wanted to say. If the trainer did know, he didn't care. That much was obvious. This wasn't personal, to Henry. It was a business decision, nothing more.

Alec went to look around for Creo, but the groom was nowhere to be found. He wasn't in his quarters in the training barn or even with Storm. Alec felt terrible. He wanted to try to explain the situation, to at least try to get the kid to understand. Actually, Alec told himself, he wished he understood the situation a little better himself.

When he returned to the office, Henry was gone. Alec sat there for a while, alone in the dark, thinking. He must have dozed off without realizing it because when he looked at his watch almost an hour had passed. Then he heard it—the familiar sound of a soft, rhythmic chant echoing up the barn corridor.

Alec looked out the doorway and saw Creo standing in front of Storm's stall, his arms around the colt's neck. He started toward them, then stopped, not wanting to interrupt. Alec thought. He turned around and walked back to the office. What was there to say? Alec knew that Creo's heart was breaking. And there was absolutely nothing anyone could do about it.

The next morning, Alec drove Creo to the diner that served as the depot for the eight o'clock bus into the city. On the way, Creo stared straight ahead, looking as uncomfortable as Alec felt. Every time Alec tried to find something appropriate to say, the words he formed in his mind sounded so phony that in the end he just gave up. *Better to not say anything than to sound like a jerk,* he told himself.

It was Creo who finally broke the silence. "Listen, Alec. Henry explained the whole thing to me."

"I bet," Alec said bitterly.

"It's business. I understand. And I've really appreciated the chance to work at Hopeful Farm. It was an experience I'll never forget."

Alec glanced over at Creo, and a pang of guilt shot through his heart. *This is too much,* Alec thought. Now the poor kid was trying to make *him* feel better.

"If there's anything I can do..." Alec began.

"I'll let you know," Creo said shortly. Alec's own disappointment was reflected in the kid's face. *It's not supposed to end this way,* Alec thought.

He pulled the truck into the diner parking lot just as the bus turned off the highway. Creo jumped out and went inside to buy his ticket. When he returned to the truck to get his bag, Alec pulled two twenty-dollar bills from his wallet and held them out to Creo.

"Here, take this," Alec said. "You might need it."

Creo refused the money, but Alec stuffed the twenties into his shirt pocket anyway. Creo glanced over his shoulders anxiously as the last few passengers were getting on the bus and reached through the truck window to shake hands with Alec.

"Take care, Creo," Alec said.

"You too. And thanks again for everything."

Creo ran to the bus and climbed aboard as it spewed a cloud of black exhaust smoke and rumbled to life. Alec reached over to roll up the passenger side window and found the two twenty-dollar bills crumpled on the seat beside him. With a heavy sigh, he picked up the bills and returned them to his wallet.

CHAPTER THIRTEEN

Drastic Measures

Without Creo for company, Storm quickly reverted to his stubborn, moody self. The colt was not above fits of kicking at his stall door or biting anyone who came close enough for him to snag. Even Deb threw up his hands, saying he was going "to keep as far away from that crazy horse as possible." Alec would never have admitted it, but even he was beginning to have his doubts about Storm.

Because of a last-minute mix-up, Creo's replacement, Pete Hartman, was unable to start work at Hopeful Farm for a few more days. That meant Henry, Alec, and Deb were right back where they'd been before Creo had arrived. A mood of quiet tension hung about the barn, and the place seemed a bit empty without the young groom around.

Aside from that, business seemed to go on pretty much as usual for the next two days. Then, on Friday afternoon, Henry caught up with Alec outside the tack room.

"Look, Alec," Henry said, "the colt just isn't ready for the Cup. I know it, and you do, too. I just talked with Stedman on the phone. He's going back to Florida tomorrow night and he's going to take Storm with him."

"Tomorrow?" Alec said, confused. "Storm's racing tomorrow!"

Henry spoke softly, but his tone was all business. "Listen, Alec. We agreed a long time ago that I'm in charge of overseeing the buying and selling around here. You're a jockey. Let's stick to our job descriptions, okay? We'll both be a lot happier."

Alec took a deep breath, trying to get his rising anger and frustration under control. "So it's like that, huh?"

"This isn't a matter of settling for the quick buck, Alec," Henry said, his voice growing even softer. "We can't afford *not* to sell Storm."

Alec's mouth dropped open. "For *five thousand dollars*? Henry, what are you doing? Are we that desperate?"

"What I'm doing is *trying* to cut our losses. Look at the way that colt's been behaving. He's just one big headache. Remember the last time you raced Storm? At Belmont? What if he goes down again on Saturday? Then where are we? After two spills in a row, no one will touch him. As I said before, five thousand dollars will just about pay us back his feed bill and half the time we've put into him."

"And what if he wins?" Alec demanded. "How many times have you told me that this business is a gamble?"

"That's right," Henry said, nodding. "And sometimes the smart move is to fold—get out of the game before you lose your shirt."

Angry, confused thoughts raced through Alec's mind. He couldn't remember the last time he'd argued with Henry like this. Alec fumed. Didn't he have *anything* to say about what happened at Hopeful Farm? Sure, Storm had problems, but you couldn't give up on a horse just like that. His intuition kept telling him that Storm possessed the one thing that no amount of training could give a racehorse—heart, the will to win.

Obviously, Henry thought otherwise. But as much as Alec respected him, he knew the old master could make mistakes the same as anyone. And Alec didn't like to be shouted at and treated like a child. He was young, but he'd paid his dues. Why couldn't Henry trust his judgment this once?

That night Alec took the Black out for a ride. It wasn't long after sundown, and a full moon was just rising over the North Ridge. Golden light brightened the hill behind the farm like the glow of a distant fire.

Alec knew he needed to sort things out. The Black felt good under him, as if he could carry Alec away from all his problems, carry him off into the starry sky. He conjured up a picture of the Black racing through the night sky, his hoofs clattering across the rings of Saturn.

Alec let the reins hang loose as the Black found a familiar path through the woods. The stallion led the way to a clearing illuminated by shafts of yellow moonlight.

"How about this spot, fella?" Alec said softly. The Black responded to his voice before he could pull up on the reins. Alec swung out of the saddle and flopped to the ground. The Black pulled away from him, lowering his head to chomp some grass.

Alec sat up and looked at the sky, absently tracing a circle in the dirt with his finger. A cool wind brushed his face as he remembered distant places and other times with the Black. Slowly his thoughts came back to earth, and to the problem of Storm.

Writing off the colt was a mistake, that much he

did know. The colt just needed a chance to prove himself. Alec couldn't really blame Henry for feeling the way he did, especially after all the trouble they'd been through with Storm, and the trainer was definitely right about one thing: They needed to win some big purses—and soon—to keep Hopeful Farm going. The expenses of both the farm and racing were tremendous. They couldn't lose money and charge it off on their tax returns the way the wealthy players who bred and raced horses for the fun of it did. If the farm didn't make a profit, they were through.

Inside his head he heard Henry, the voice of long experience, saying, "*Get professional. Stick to your job description...*"

But what did that mean, exactly? Alec knew that he was more to Hopeful Farm than strong legs and light hands. *Yeah, try to tell Henry that,* he thought. Lately, Henry had been treating him as if it wasn't his job to think.

It hadn't always been that way, Alec recalled. Despite his decades-long advantage over Alec as a horseman, Henry usually gave his jockey credit for having a head on his shoulders, especially when it came to horses. If nothing else, Henry generally trusted Alec's intuition with the horses he exercised, his opinions about what they could do and what they couldn't. The trust between him and Henry had helped build Hopeful Farm into what it was today. That trust set Henry apart from people like Luke Stedman, who saw only the youth in Alec's face.

Their mutual love of horses had always been a bond between Alec and Henry, bridging the gap of years. Now it seemed that Henry was having second thoughts about trusting Alec's judgment—at least as far as Black Storm was concerned.

It just didn't seem fair, especially after all the races he'd won for Hopeful Farm and all the winners he'd helped them produce. *Why do I always have to keep proving myself?* Alec thought. Then again, it didn't really surprise him that much. There was a saying around the jockeys' room: "You're only as good as your last race." It was the same for just about anyone. In the end, all he had—all *anyone* really had—was his self-respect...and his dreams.

Suddenly, the nebulous idea that had been floating along the edges of his consciousness came sharply into focus, like a name he'd been trying to remember.

Maybe there *was* a way for Storm to run on Saturday. Maybe they could still make it if...

Alec swallowed hard. It was a crazy idea. Dangerous. Risky. But it just might pay off. Alec whistled to the Black, jumped into the saddle, and turned the stallion home.

Half an hour later, Alec was in the training barn office talking on the phone to Brooklyn.

"Back up a second there, Alec," said Creo, on the other end of the line. "What you said about 'borrowing' Storm, you really mean stealing, right?"

"I'd be stealing from myself, if you want to look at it that way," Alec said. "By all rights, Storm's still a Hopeful Farm colt. The deal with Stedman can't go through with no horse to sell, that's all. It's not stealing, exactly."

"But technically he still belongs to Henry?" Creo tried to follow Alec's logic.

"Hopeful Farm, Incorporated. That's my folks and Henry, yeah. Legally I can't own any part of the farm *and* ride the horses at the same time."

"So that means..."

Alec was getting impatient now. "Listen, man, I'm talking about saving Storm," he said, his words hot and quick. "Are you going to help me out or not? We just need a place to spend the night."

"Well, Mace might not go for it," Creo said slowly. "But, sure, I'll talk to him."

Alec hung up the phone and sat back in his

chair. Trying to collect his thoughts, he took a pen and piece of paper from the desk drawer and wrote a letter to Henry explaining what he was doing and why. Halfway through, he tore the letter up. He wasn't certain *he* understood what he was doing. When he started putting everything into words, it really *didn't* make any sense.

Finally, he settled on a short note that read simply, "*Taking Storm for a day off. Please don't worry. I know what I'm doing. See you tomorrow night.*" He put the note in the top drawer of the desk, a place where he knew Henry would find it, but probably not right away.

Suddenly, Alec caught sight of something in the window. A chill shot through him. *Henry!* Alec jumped to his feet, almost knocking over his chair. After a moment, his heart pounding wildly, he realized what he'd seen in the window was just his own reflection in the glass.

Breathing a sigh of relief, Alec crept quietly from the barn. His conscience was still heavy and his mind continued to play tricks on him. He heard footsteps behind him and imagined seeing Henry in every shadow. Trying to shove those thoughts aside, Alec ran out to the van and pulled it quickly around to the front of the barn. Then he went to Storm's stall, opened the door and walked Storm outside.

Deb must have heard them, because his head suddenly poked out the window of his apartment in the loft of the barn.

"Need any help, Alec?" Deb called sleepily.

"Uh, no, that's okay, Deb."

The groom saw Storm and seemed to realize what Alec was doing. He let out a low whistle. "What the heck are you up to, anyway?"

"Please, Deb. Everything's fine. Go back to your TV show, will you?"

Deb mumbled something, but his head disappeared back inside the barn.

Soon Alec was turning the van onto the county road that led to the highway, feeling like a thief in the night. Technically, Alec kept reminding himself, he wasn't stealing. Legally, the colt still belonged to Hopeful Farm, despite whatever deal Henry had made with Stedman. No sale could be finalized with Storm unaccounted for. And in the meantime, Storm could run in the Gold Cup wearing Hopeful Farm colors.

I have to trust in myself, Alec thought. *And in Storm.* But why did doing something that was supposed to be right feel so wrong? He could only hope that everything would go well and that Henry would understand in the end.

Alec gazed out the van window at the pearly lights strung along the New York State Thruway. The waves of doubt washing over him now were becoming almost unbearable. *There's still time to turn around and take Storm back to the farm,* he thought. *If I hurry, Henry will never be the wiser.*

But then what? He'd just go to bed and watch Stedman drive off with Storm tomorrow? *No way.*

CHAPTER FOURTEEN

Skyway

Around midnight, Alec found himself winding the van through the streets of East Gunnery, hoping he could remember the way to Mace's stable. He pulled to a stop at a traffic light in front of a fast-food hamburger place, across the street from a boarded-up gas station. Three kids were sitting in a black van with the doors open and a tape deck blaring, looking hard at Alec. A wary chill stiffened his back.

Following Gunnery Street, Alec pulled into the old, deserted-looking lumberyard off Z Street. A light was on in the stable. Alec parked the van and went inside. Mace was leaning back in an office chair, listening to a sports-talk radio program. The stable owner looked as if he was half asleep, his cowboy hat pulled down low on his forehead.

Alec cleared his throat.

Mace sat up. "Who's that?"

"Alec Ramsay. Sorry. Did I scare you?"

The stocky ex-boxer shook his head, giving Alec the once-over with his piercing gray eyes. "I don't scare easy," said Mace. "Sometimes I get curious, though. And right now I'm curious about what you're doing here. Creo ran this whole thing by me, but I want to hear it from you."

Alec glanced around hopefully. "Is Creo here?"

"He stepped out to the store for a minute. I sent him for juice."

Mace leaned back and crossed his arms behind his head as if he had all the time in the world.

Alec took a deep breath. "I have Storm in the van. We'd like to stay here tonight. That is, if you'll let us."

"So Creo said. I've been thinking about that." There was a long pause. "You wanna help me decide?"

"If I can."

"Tell me what this whole thing is about. And don't try to smoke me."

Alec frowned. "I wouldn't do that."

"You mean you *couldn't* do that. Out with it, Mr. Ramsay."

Mace listened to Alec's story with an even gaze,

nodding slowly at intervals. He didn't interrupt, letting Alec pause now and then in mid-sentence to search for words. As Alec had promised, everything he told Mace was the truth, although he didn't go into every detail. Alec tried to find a delicate balance, telling the big man enough to satisfy his curiosity, but not so much as to make him accountable if anything went wrong.

Creo came back from the store carrying a quart of orange juice. He handed it to Mace and stood quietly beside Alec.

When Alec was finished with his story, Mace leaned forward, resting his elbows on the arms of his chair. "You done?" Mace asked.

Alec nodded.

"Something tells me there's more to this than you're letting on."

"I swear every word is the truth."

"I'm sure."

Alec reached for his back pocket. "Listen, I'll pay whatever..."

Mace raised one hand, signaling Alec to stop. Deep furrows creased his forehead. "If I help you out, son, it won't be for the money," he said, his chest swelling angrily. "And that's a real big *if*."

Alec took another deep breath and waited. The tone of Mace's voice carried a hint of finality. *This is it,* thought Alec. *Either we go or we stay.* He glanced at Creo, who also seemed to be holding his breath, then back at Mace again.

After what felt like an eternity to Alec, the big cowboy stood up and straightened his hat. He threw Creo a sober, near-threatening look. "I'm going to Boo's place awhile. Then I'm going home. Creo, I'm leaving you in charge here, understand?"

Creo gave a slight nod. Alec nearly collapsed in relief.

"Thank you, Mace," said Alec. "You don't know what this means to me."

Mace walked to the door. "To tell you the truth, I'm thinking of the colt," he said. "Storm shouldn't be spending the night in that van."

Alec and Creo quickly set Storm up in an empty stall in one of the sheds. Creo spent the night on a cot outside the stall while Alec made a bed for himself in the back of the van. With so much on his mind, Alec found it impossible to fall asleep. By the time he did finally manage to close his eyes, it was almost time to get up again.

At dawn, Alec pushed open the half-doors of the van. *This is it,* he thought. *Race day.* As he reached to pick a piece of straw from his hair, he heard a voice coming from the shed. He walked inside and found

Creo talking to Storm. The colt shook his head restlessly.

"This guy needs airing out," Creo said. "How about we hit the skyway?"

Alec hestitated. "Come on, Alec. When am I going to get another chance to ride Storm? It's Saturday, and it's still early. There's no traffic."

Alec glanced at his watch. "Okay, sure. Why not?"

Creo brought Storm and Tina, Mace's venerable old mare, out of their stalls. Alec slipped the bridle over Tina's small head. "Hey there, girl. How've you been? Did you miss me?" He ran his hand across the warm place between the fall of the mare's mane and her smooth, firm neck.

Alec and Creo walked their horses the few blocks to the on-ramp of the unpaved highway above the streets. Creo and Storm led the way around the barricade, up the ramp, and out onto the span of stubbled grass and graded dirt.

"It's like a different world up here," Alec said. "I wonder how long they're going to leave this place as it is."

"Mace says it could be years before anything changes up here, with the budget cuts and all."

Alec laughed. "Well, that's one benefit of life in the city."

As they cantered by the clifflike high-rise towers crowding the skyway, Storm's clear, high neigh rang out through the still morning air.

"Take it easy," Alec warned Creo. "Storm has a big day ahead of him."

The kid gave a nod and a wave, then broke Storm into a gallop for half a mile before turning back.

Gazing around, Alec wondered whether every horse lover had some magical place, at least in their dreams. Maybe for Storm and Creo it was right here, high above the Brooklyn streets.

A warm wind began to rise as the riders left the skyway behind. Alec glanced over his shoulder one last time at the span of unpaved road rising above the rooftops. Seagulls circled overhead as the city slowly began to show signs of life.

Back at the stable, Mace's students hadn't shown up yet for their early morning riding lessons. The place was still quiet. Mace was puttering around in the tack room. He came out to greet Alec and Creo as they returned from their ride.

"Good morning!" Mace boomed. "Did you all sleep okay?"

"Fine, thanks," Alec replied, giving Mace a sleepy smile. *He certainly seems in a better mood this morning,* he thought.

"Mace, do you think it'd be all right if I went with Alec today?" Creo asked. "He's going to need some help with the colt."

Mace frowned. "I thought you were all through working for Hopeful Farm."

"Come on, Mace," Creo pleaded. "It's just for one day. I'll work here overtime every day next week if you want me to."

"That's all right, Creo," the stable owner replied with a sigh. "I know how you feel about that colt. You go ahead."

"Thanks, Mace."

The big man's voice softened. "You know, as a matter of fact, I have some business in Philly that I've been putting off for weeks. Maybe I'll take a drive down there this afternoon and stop by the race on my way home. I'd like to see the colt race, too."

"That'd be great," Alec said. "They sent me some extra tickets with my stable pass. I'll get you one." He jogged to the van, found a ticket in the glove compartment, and gave it to Mace.

"Thanks, Alec," the stable owner said. "I've never been to a steeplechase before. It sounds like fun."

Alec laughed. "Actually, I've only been to a few myself," he admitted.

Storm was given a quick grooming and loaded

into the van again. With a wave to Mace, Alec threw the van into gear and set their course for the Gold Cup. A solitary witness, Mace's black-and-white nanny goat, wandered around the side of a shed and stared after them.

CHAPTER FIFTEEN

Stedman's Game

The van rattled up the driveway, past crumbling loading docks and around the side of the lumberyard. After driving a few short blocks through the deserted industrial section, Alec turned onto the neighborhood streets of East Gunnery. Soon, they were rolling along the New Jersey interstate, headed for Pennsylvania.

As he drove, Alec's thoughts turned once again to the race. He had only a vague idea of who would be the other entries in the Cup race. Without a doubt, he would be facing many seasoned competitors. He wondered if he would recognize any of them from Belmont or Aqueduct. Maybe not. In the United States, steeplechasers and flat trackers rarely mixed.

Alec swallowed hard and felt a flutter of nervousness run down his spine. *So many things could go wrong,* he thought. The risk factors multiplied with every unknown—and there were plenty of question marks in this situation. He could only hope that all the training Storm had been through back at the farm would pay off.

I need to keep a positive attitude, Alec told himself. He had to psych himself up, not out. A major case of nerves wouldn't do him any good right now. Besides, he'd be getting the answers to all of his questions soon enough.

Two hours later, Alec, Creo, and Storm reached Searsdale, a town of Colonial-style mansions surrounded by a felt-green sea of grass. The road to Chandler Field, the site of the Pennsylvania Gold Cup, snaked through well-tended pastures. Low stone walls crisscrossed the fields on either side of the road.

Arriving at the Cup grounds, they found the mile-long hurdle course set up in a meadow. It was bordered by wide lawns on one side and thick woods on the other. Alec slowed the van to a crawl and followed a line of horse trailers around to the stable area.

Alec fished around in the glove compartment for the stable pass he'd received in the mail after paying Storm's entrance fee, and he held it up to the security guard at the stable entrance. The guard eyed Alec and Creo suspiciously, then nodded them through the gate.

After unloading Storm, Creo led the colt around to the perimeter of the stable area, letting him walk off the ride. Instead of the usual barns, long, wide tents containing temporary stalls were being used to house the horses. Alec went to check in at the steward's stand adjoining the paddock.

As he walked along the railing, Alec surveyed the track, noting the condition of the turf. By all accounts, this was a good galloping course that would suit Storm perfectly. A chestnut filly cantered past, ridden by an official wearing a checked jacket, black boots, and riding breeches.

Adjoining the official's stand was a single low bleacher in front of the finish line. It was quite a change from the towering metal-tiered grandstands at Belmont or any of the other tracks to which Alec was accustomed. There was an almost country club feel to the place. Even the course was different from the usual oval racetrack. It cut an oblong, kidney-shaped path through a grassy meadow and a large group of spreading oaks.

After checking in and picking up Storm's numbered saddle cloth, Alec saw that the colt was going off from the number 7 position in a field of twelve. *Right in the middle of the pack,* Alec thought. A slot more on the outside would have been nice, but that was life.

The Gold Cup was the feature race of the day devoted exclusively to steeplechasing. It would be the fifth of seven races to be run over this course, two full circuits. The distance from start to finish was two miles, a bit short compared to most steeplechase courses.

From the vantage point of the steward's stand, Alec could view the entire grounds, the racecourse, and the beautifully manicured countryside. Behind the stands in the other direction, more early arrivals were milling about on the wide lawns. Some were already camped out along the rail. A line of colorful hospitality tents, reserved for the race sponsors and their guests, was pitched farther beyond the stands.

Back at the stables once again, Alec walked the length of the tent barn to Storm's box stall. Creo was talking with one of the other grooms, a lanky man wearing denim overalls.

"Hey, Creo," Alec said as he came up. "I'll stay with Storm for a while. Why don't you take a break?"

Creo shrugged. "No, that's okay, thanks."

Alec wondered whether the young kid from Brooklyn was feeling a bit self-conscious. "Don't worry about how you're dressed," Alec said. "We're part of the show. Most of those guys in jackets and ties are just here to socialize."

"Maybe I *will* take a walk around the infield," Creo said, "just to see how the course is laid out."

"Go ahead," Alec told him. "We still have plenty of time. The first race won't start for a while, and the Gold Cup won't go off till the fifth."

When Creo left, Alec sat down on a tack trunk and folded back the racing program. He wanted to look at the past performances for each horse in the race. Storm's stats looked pretty meager. He was the only three-year-old, too. At least they'd been given a weight advantage against the more seasoned horses.

An hour later, the lawns around Chandler Field were swarming with people. The first race was about to start. Alec took another stroll to check out the action. As he passed the corporate tents, he could see the men in summer suits and fashionable women crowded together inside, dining at long banquet tables and chatting among themselves. Alec knew that their money was revitalizing the steeplechase circuit in the United States—fortunately with a minimum of commercialization. Today, executives representing luxury cars, newspapers, communications companies, and a host of other sponsors were holding court in their private tents while the Chandler

Hunt Club looked after the racing end of the affair.

Beyond the clusters of tents, formal tailgate parties and picnics were in full swing out in the trackside parking area. Seeing all the delicious-looking spreads of food was making Alec hungry. All he and Creo had had for breakfast was a couple of doughnuts they'd picked up at a gas station on the road. Alec put all thoughts of food out of his mind. He never liked to ride on a full stomach, anyway.

Alec watched the first race, an amateur steeplechase, then wandered back toward the stable area. Stepping through the gate, he was startled to see someone waiting for him outside of Storm's tent.

It was Luke Stedman, wearing an aloof expression that he probably thought went well with his expensive-looking suit. Alec's stomach churned nervously. *Calm down,* he told himself. *No matter what he says, Storm still belongs to Hopeful Farm.*

"Mr. Stedman," Alec greeted him. "What a surprise. What are you doing here?"

"Me?" Stedman asked. A toothy grin worked its way across his tanned face. "Shouldn't *I* be asking *you* that question, Ramsay? I came looking for my colt. Henry guessed you might have brought him here. I spoke to him on the phone about an hour ago. I must say, he didn't sound very happy. I imagine he's on his way here right now."

"*Your* colt?" Alec blurted out.

"That's right," Stedman said. "Mine."

Alec swallowed hard. "I never agreed to sell Storm to you."

Stedman scratched his chin as if he were considering Alec's words. "Are *you* in charge of the buying and selling at Hopeful Farm? I thought that was Henry's job."

Alec flushed. "It's partly Henry's job, yes. And partly mine, too—at least in Storm's case."

"So you're saying Storm belongs to you?"

Alec didn't answer.

"The last time I read the rules governing this sort of thing, it was illegal for an owner to ride one of his own horses in a race."

Suddenly, Alec understood Stedman was right! How could he be so stupid?

Stedman bore down for the kill. "Even if you're only *part* owner, you can't race Storm. You'll be disqualified. So what exactly do you think you're doing here?"

Stall for time, Alec told himself, trying not to panic. He had to think. *I have to think.*

Stedman's eyes glinted savagely. "Let's cut out the games, Ramsay," he went on in that intimidating tone. "Henry gave me the okay to take Storm. The only way you're going to stop me is by acknowledging that you own him. If you do that, I'll just go have a little talk with the race officials and you won't be riding him anywhere. So what's it going to be? Are you the owner or the jockey? You can't have it both ways."

Alec felt the heat of anger rising up inside him. "Give me a break, Mr. Stedman." he said. "Don't you have enough horseflesh to worry about? What is Storm to you?"

"An investment, nothing more." The trainer sounded almost uninterested. "But I'm very particular about my investments." His voice hardened. "You made a big mistake, Ramsay. You didn't know what you were getting into when you decided to tangle with me."

Images raced through Alec's mind: *Henry. Storm. Creo.* He stood there helplessly, trying to retain a shell of composure. Then, suddenly, an idea came to him. Maybe Stedman had given him the very answer he needed.

"Wait here just a minute, Mr. Stedman," Alec said. "I want you to meet someone."

He ran to the stall where Creo was giving Storm a last minute grooming. "Something's come up, Creo," he said breathlessly. "How would you feel about racing Storm?"

Creo looked up from his brush. "I'd really like to do that someday."

"I'm not talking about *some*day, Creo," Alec said urgently. "I mean *now*."

Creo looked stunned. "*Now?* You're telling me I get to ride on Storm? Today?"

"If you want it."

"But why? I don't get it. After all you went through to get Storm here, why give *me* the ride?"

Alec lowered his voice. "Stedman's here."

"So?" Creo asked, still confused. "I thought you said..."

"He's threatening to take Storm. At the very least, he can stop me from riding the colt today. But Storm needs this race, and I'll have to go on record as part owner. That means someone else gets the ride. How about it?" Alec raised his eyebrows. "Are you ready?"

"Oh, man," Creo said. "You know I am!"

"And I know you can do it," Alec told him. "Someone has to tap Storm for that will to win. To tell you the truth, I'm figuring your chances are better than mine."

Together they walked back to Storm's stall. "Okay, Mr. Stedman," Alec said. "You said the only way I could stop you from taking Storm was to give up the ride. Well, then, I will. *This* is the jockey who will be riding Storm."

Stedman stared at Creo and burst out laughing. "*Him?* Your groom? You're getting a little desperate, don't you think?"

"He has a galloping license," Alec said flatly.

"Ever ridden in a steeplechase before, son?" Stedman asked Creo.

"No, sir," Creo admitted.

"How about a regular flat-track race?"

Creo didn't answer this time. He looked down at the ground. Stedman turned back to Alec. "You're really serious, aren't you?"

"Completely," Alec said.

Stedman started laughing again and then finally caught his breath. "So you're telling me that the ride on this colt, who has thrown you every time you've raced him, is going to some kid who has never even ridden in a low-priced claiming race?"

"Don't worry too much about it, Mr. Stedman," Alec said. "You'll have to excuse us, please. We have a race to get ready for."

"Oh, *I'm* not worrying," the trainer said. "But maybe *you* should be. Henry Dailey is certainly going to enjoy hearing about this when he gets here. I think I just might wait around to see what he has to say. I'd sure hate to miss the fireworks."

CHAPTER SIXTEEN

Stepping Up

Alec paced nervously outside Storm's tent. *If Henry shows up now, I'll have to do some real fast talking,* he thought. But post time for the Gold Cup was quickly approaching. Creo had already headed out to the van to change into the silks Alec had brought with him.

A few moments later, Creo came striding back, wearing Hopeful Farm's racing colors, a huge grin spread wide across his face. He turned to Alec. "Do I look cool or what?"

Alec inspected the plastic riding goggles for smudges and smiled. "Yeah, you'll pass."

"Ha!" Creo spun around and shuffled his feet in a little victory dance. Then he checked out his reflection again in the side-view mirror of a nearby car.

As Creo started toward the official's stand to have the assigned weight added to his saddle, Alec heard a deep, familiar voice. Mace had arrived! "What are you doing in those silks, Creo?" the stable owner boomed.

"You won't believe this, Mace," Creo said. Quickly, he explained the situation. Mace listened quietly, the shocked expression on his face slowly giving way to suspicion.

"This could be my big break, Mace," Creo finished.

"*Or* it could explode in your face. Then what?"

"Creo has the talent and the ability," Alec jumped in. "And I have the horse."

"You do?"

Alec tried not to sound too defensive. "Well, I know Storm's ownership status is a bit...uh, questionable at the moment. But..."

"You know, Creo was doing just fine back in Brooklyn before you and Storm showed up," Mace began.

"Believe me," said Alec, trying to sound confident, "everything will work out once we prove what Storm can really do. I guarantee it."

Mace shook his head incredulously. "You really don't understand, do you, Alec? Don't you realize that if Creo starts crossing people like your Henry

Dailey and this Stedman character, his career at the track is over even before it starts?"

"It's not gonna be like that, Mace," Alec said hotly.

Mace crossed his arms. "You don't know a thing about how it's gonna be."

"Hey, Mace," Creo broke in. "Lighten up, man."

Mace turned his dark glare from Alec to Creo.

"C'mon, Mace," Creo went on. "What are you getting all down on Alec for? I'm willing to take the risk."

Mace gazed at Alec and Creo for a long moment, then sighed heavily. "I guess no one could tell me anything when I was your age, either."

"Try to understand, Mace," Creo said.

"Oh, I understand, all right. I just want to make sure *you* understand what you're getting yourself into. This isn't going to be like your workouts at that farm upstate. There's going to be traffic and..."

"You're making me nervous, Mace," Creo broke in, putting a hand on the big man's shoulder. "Go find a place by the rail, will you?"

Mace shook his head and turned away. "I'll be rooting for you, kid."

Alec and Creo watched as Mace disappeared into the crowd outside the stable area.

"Don't mind him," Creo said.

"He sounds a lot like Henry," Alec said. "He's just worried about you."

Creo nodded. "We're just lucky he didn't start in on his 'I've been to the mountaintop' sermon. We'd be standing here until nightfall."

Alec chuckled. Then he grew serious and looked Creo straight in the eye. "In a way he's right, though. You're taking a risk. And I hope you know that you don't owe me a thing. I have to feel certain that you want to do this."

"I do, Alec, more than anything. This ride is for me and Storm, no one else."

Alec took charge of the colt as Creo carried the saddle and saddle cloth to the official's stand to weigh in. They were lucky about one thing, Alec told himself. The weights the horses were allowed to carry in a steeplechase, including the jockey, were much higher than in flat-track racing. Because Storm was a lightly raced three-year-old, he would be carrying less than the rest of the field.

With the saddle and cloth in his arms, Creo stepped up on the scales and waited as the official inserted extra weight bars in the saddle. The needle stopped at 136 pounds.

"That's fine, Chase," the clerk of the scales said. "You can get down now." Creo did as he was told.

"Next!" the clerk called out.

Alec led Storm to the paddock. The colt looked over the field, his gaze fixed above Alec's head. So far, the colt's behavior had been excellent. The magic that Creo always worked with Storm seemed to be holding.

"Attention, please," a voice crackled over the loudspeaker. "There will be a change of jockeys for the fifth race. Hopeful Farm's Black Storm will now be ridden by Creo Chase. Ten minutes to post time."

Once in the saddling area, Alec had a chance to get a good look at the other horses in the Gold Cup. Like their jockeys, they were a mixed bag. First there was Interpol, the war-horse, a top money winner and proven vet of the hunt club circuit. According to the racing program, the California-bred stallion had taken last year's Gold Cup with a commanding victory. For almost the entire two miles, even after twelve jumps, he'd kept the lead. Interpol's chief rival for favorite status today was front-running Heavenly, a five-year-old mare sired by turf wizard Heaventeen. Both horses were being saddled by topnotch trainers and ridden by professional jockeys.

There were several other pro riders in the field, as well as some highly skilled and experienced amateurs. Neither the cinnamon-skinned mare For Real nor the lightly raced Kikkoman could boast better than mediocre performances at the local tracks, but both were bred for distance. Alec also recognized Chazz and his jockey, Tom Hall, from Alec's disastrous steeplechase at Belmont last month—the race Chazz had gone on to win.

It was plain to see that the competition at American steeplechases was stiffening in proportion to the escalating amounts of purse money. Nonetheless, almost half of the horses in today's field were being ridden by amateurs, one or two of whom looked soft, slightly overweight, and nervous.

One young jockey glanced at Creo and whispered something to another jockey beside him. They cast disdainful glances at Creo and Storm, not seeming to care whether Creo noticed. A few other riders joined in appraising the rookie as well. Alec hoped that Creo would hang tough. Confidence—and attitude—were key factors in any race.

Tom Hall strode over to Alec and Creo and made the effort to say hello. Creo returned a cautious smile.

Hall nodded at the snickering jockeys. "Don't pay attention to those clowns, pal. They're just trying to rattle you," he said. "You have as good a shot as any of us."

"Thanks," Creo said. "But don't you worry. We don't scare so easy where I come from. And I think I just might have the horse to beat today."

Hall gave a good-natured laugh. "That's the way, kid."

Twenty yards away, Interpol's trainer, Kevin Bartelme, was talking to his top-rated jockey, Sylvester Santos. Bartelme glanced over at Storm and Creo, his face tightening as he recognized Hopeful Farm's colors on Storm. It was doubtful they were dismissing the colt's chances as easily as everyone else, but confidence in their own horse seemed fully justified. The big gray stallion held his head high, his ears pricked forward.

Alec gazed around. Mace must have found himself a spot to watch the race down by the rail. Stedman was standing outside the saddling area, probably watching them and waiting for Henry to show up.

Still no sign of Henry, Alec thought. *If we can just get through the next few minutes...*

He and Creo huddled together for a quick review of race strategy. Creo's face held a mixture of great anticipation and the first few hints of nervousness.

"Remember," Alec instructed, "keep clear of the pack. Chances are the rest of the field will be trying to save ground along the inside rail. Ease out when you can."

Creo nodded. They both knew that, after the previous four races, the condition of the turf on the outside would be firmer, even though it would mean a slightly longer distance around.

"When you do have to move between horses," Alec added, "make sure you do it quickly in case a horse goes down in front of you."

Creo nodded again, but his attention was focused on Interpol. The kid was clearly impressed. "Don't worry about him," Alec said, "or Heavenly, either. Don't worry about *any* of them. You only have to worry about one horse: Yours."

Creo slid his hand across Storm's neck and gave the colt a pat, obviously eager to get going.

"Hey, this is new for me, too," Alec told him. "I'm usually the one sitting in the saddle listening to all the instructions. How do you feel?"

Creo kept stroking Storm's neck. "I've been waiting for this moment all my life. How am I supposed to feel?"

Alec slapped him on the back. "This is your time, Creo. Yours and Storm's. I know you two can step up. Good luck."

Creo waved as Alec sent him after the others to the track. Across the course, a crowd was now moving away from the paddock and saddle areas to take up a favored vantage point for the race. The low bleacher was packed, but there was still standing room along the rail.

Alec squeezed into a place beside the rail. Once again, he glanced at the names and past performances of the horses listed in his program. Despite the presence of the two favorites and the other well-bred unknowns, the Gold Cup stacked up as anybody's race. From the looks of the racing form, at least four of the horses had an excellent shot at winning. And then, of course, there was Storm.

The field of twelve made its way down to parade in front of the official's stand. Heading the line, the champion Interpol looked like a horse for whom the Pennsylvania Gold Cup, with all its excitement and drama, was a natural home. Storm was looking pretty good as well, his nostrils flared and ears pricked. The extra conditioning at Hopeful Farm had left him in superb shape.

Alec raised his binoculars, feeling a brief pang of envy. As glad as he was to see Creo out there on Storm, he knew deep in his heart that he'd rather be riding the colt himself. But he also knew that Creo was the one for the job today.

Alec gazed across the green splendor of Chandler Field. Brush hurdles about four feet high dotted the oblong course at furlong intervals. He watched as the jockeys milled back and forth on their mounts, killing time chatting as they waited to line up for the start. Creo kept to himself, leaning forward in his saddle to rub Storm behind the ears.

When post time arrived, Alec was dismayed to see that Storm refused to join the rest of the field at the line. Alec gripped the binoculars a little tighter, adjusting the focus. The other horses made room for Storm's overeager dancing, their jocks grumbling about the holdup in the start caused by an unruly colt and his apprentice rider. Creo gave Storm a cross kick in the ribs. The colt put his ears back and looked sour.

Two assistant starters tried to push Storm from behind and came close to being kicked in the face for their trouble. After some discussion, the two burly men led Storm forward a few paces, then backed him into position. It worked, but to Alec the delay seemed to take forever.

Finally, all the horses were lined up and ready to start. Alec could see Creo pulling his goggles down over his face. Alec took a deep breath.

The starters waved their flags, and the horses surged in front of the official's stand, the thunder of their steel-shod hoofs rumbling the ground.

The racecourse commentator's voice crackled over the loudspeaker: "And they're off!"

CHAPTER SEVENTEEN

Photo Finish!

It was a clean break. Storm, even after his disruptive antics at the start, charged out, the first of the field into his stride. Creo moved Storm slightly wide, without close company to the left or right and no one in front of him.

The horses bore down on the first hurdle with clods of earth flying through the air like shrapnel. For one awkward moment, Alec thought Storm alone would set the pace, but as the colt neared the hurdle, the copper-colored Heavenly surged ahead with John Burke set firmly in the irons. Burke flattened himself over Heavenly's withers, already giving her rein. They hit the first jump and soared over the brush as if they were skipping over a crack in the sidewalk.

Next it was Creo's turn. Using hands and heels,

Creo kept Storm together, and the colt sailed easily into his next stride. Then came the mare For Real and the big gray Interpol, with Ridge-Runner close on his heels.

As he left the first hurdle behind, Interpol blasted by Storm on the inside with For Real running hot in his slipstream. More runners pushed past Storm on the inside. Alec gave a sigh of relief. The race was becoming a procession, and Creo had the sense to let Storm settle in toward the rear, with only a couple of horses behind him now. *Good,* Alec thought. The outside position gave Creo a better view of the hurdles to come.

The field of horses took to the next hurdle, then disappeared behind some trees. A low hill in the center of the course blocked the race from view. When the stampede came into sight again, the field was divided into two groups, separated by nearly fifteen lengths. At this point there were no stragglers.

The commentator's voice was unemotional and reserved, with a clipped British accent. "As they pass the half, it's Interpol in front now, who's made every yard of the running, behind him a group of horses led by Kikkoman. Keller is in good position on For Real. Heavenly and Black Storm have dropped way back. Chazz has yet to move. Ridge-Runner has an awful lot still to do..."

After the next hurdle, Lenny Keller, For Real's jockey, let the big mare have the bit, and she took the lead from the front runners. Chazz bounded along at the head of the second group under heavy pressure from Black Storm. The front runners turned for home. After the blistering early pace, Alec knew, everything would change soon. That was when the race would begin in earnest.

Sure enough, as the horses passed the crowd at the mile marker and set off for a second circuit over the course, the sprint between the first few hurdles began to tell on the leaders. Six lengths behind them, Storm was running with confidence, lengthening his stride and making up time between jumps.

Alec began to feel hopeful. Creo was smart enough to recognize the excellent position he was in. All he had to do now was wait until the leaders started falling behind. By the time the front runners woke up to the fact that a horse they had discounted was galloping as strongly as ever, ears pricked, it just might be too late.

Around the far turn they came. Individually or in groups of twos and threes, the rush of horses began to clear the second-to-last hurdle. In the outside third-place position, Storm strode powerfully along, a few lengths behind the soon-to-be-retired leaders, Kikkoman and Chazz.

The Hopeful Farm colt hit the front with less than a quarter of a mile to the finish. He moved into the straight. Only one more hurdle to go!

Storm drove hard at the brush, gathered himself, and with virtually no pause in stride, began to lift off the turf and soar. Then came Interpol, showing incredible stamina and close enough to mount a final charge to the wire. Within seconds, the gray warhorse was clipping Storm's heels.

Slowly but steadily, the Gold Cup champion inched up on Creo's inside. Alec gripped his binoculars. Now was the time for Creo to really keep his cool. Storm flattened his ears and drew down on the finish, kicking into overdrive with what seemed like very little urging from Creo. Interpol answered back by bumping up his speed another notch.

Race fever swept through the crowd packing the rails. A tremendous roar swelled with the thunder of approaching hoofs. Interpol and Black Storm entered the final furlong running neck and neck, their riders elbow to elbow. Beside Creo, Santos was pushing and kicking Interpol for all he was worth, waving his whip like an orchestra conductor winding up for the big finish.

"Into the last furlong," the racetrack announcer called, "and it's Interpol by a nose. Black Storm is still hanging in there. It looks to be between these two. But here comes Heavenly, absolutely flying on the inside. A terrific challenge from Heavenly, now matching Interpol and Black Storm stride for stride..."

Heavenly hit the front. Storm pushed ahead again, and Interpol followed suit, pulling away by a half-length under the whip. Heavenly couldn't take the pressure and slowly drifted back.

Storm's eyes were ablaze, his teeth bare. Once again, Creo pulled elbow to elbow with Santos. Interpol moved a head in front with less than half a furlong to the wire. He seemed to have his race won, but Storm still kept struggling to get back at him. Only now, Creo seemed to be urging Storm on, crouched and rocking low over Storm's neck, his head buried in the flying black mane.

Suddenly, it was not a question of by how much Interpol would take his second Gold Cup, but whether he could hold on to win at all. The horses charged the final few strides to the finish line and rushed by. The thunder of hoofs and the huge roar of the crowd drowned out the voice crackling over the loudspeaker. Finally, the announcer broke through the noise.

"At the wire it was very close, but I think it was Black Storm who took it by a nod. There will be a photo, but there's not much doubt about the winner:

Black Storm, ridden with breathtaking confidence by the young apprentice Creo Chase, who got up in the last stride to..."

Alec let loose, hooting and jumping up and down. "Yes! Yes! Yes!" he shouted. All around him, people were on their feet applauding. Voices buzzing everywhere. Already Storm's victory was being called the greatest Cup finish in years.

A reporter recognized Alec and called his name. But Alec wasn't ready to talk to the press just yet. He turned away and began to push his way through the crowd toward the winner's circle.

Storm slowed to a canter, then a trot. A photograph was announced, but everyone already knew the result. Creo stood in his stirrups, one fist raised in the air victoriously. Then he began patting Storm's neck excitedly. Both horse and jockey looked exhausted.

Sylvester Santos cantered up astride Storm on Interpol. He pulled down his goggles and extended an open hand. "Congratulations, Chase," he said. Creo smacked palms with Sylvester, then turned the colt through the gap to face the throng in the winner's circle.

Another rousing cheer went up as the two of them entered the enclosure. The colt drew back, giving his head a slight shake. Despite all the clamor, he did not fight his rider. Alec took Storm by the halter and someone put a horseshoe of yellow roses around the colt's neck. Storm sprang back slightly, but then stood still to nobly accept his laurels.

Cameras began to flash as journalists scribbled notes on their pads. Creo dismounted to weigh in, staggering slightly as he touched ground. Streaks of sweat and grime smeared his face. The impression left by the goggles on his face made him look like an owl. He took his saddle and stepped up on the scales. Swiftly, the results were announced as official.

Back in the winner's circle a few moments later, Creo and Alec pounded each other on the back and began talking simultaneously.

"You did it! You did it!" Alec cried as he tossed a cooler over Storm's back.

Creo's eyes shone. "Somebody tell me I'm not dreaming."

Alec gave Storm an affectionate pat. "Does this colt have heart or what?"

"Did you see the way he came back at Interpol for the stretch drive?" Creo asked excitedly. "That was *so* beautiful!" Storm tossed his head as Alec and Creo both began pressing the colt with caresses.

Alec smiled and thought of the Black. "His daddy sure will be proud of him today."

"Beginner's luck," Creo joked.

"That's what they'll say, all right," Alec said.

"Well, let 'em."

They both laughed. Storm kept bobbing his head, prancing in place. Creo leaned up next to him and for a while both of them reveled in all the attention. Everyone in the crowd was still exclaiming about the tremendous finish.

The lieutenant governor of Pennsylvania was on hand to present the trophy and the check. He was flanked by the vice president of some big corporation, a movie star Alec had never heard of, and a former shortstop for the Philadelphia Phillies. They all squeezed together for the official photograph with Black Storm. Mace looked on proudly from behind a guard rope. Stedman was nowhere to be seen. *Where is Henry?* Alec wondered suddenly. *Did he miss the race?*

Finally, the ceremony was through. The crowd cheered again as Storm whinnied and threw his head high in the air. The sports reporters wanted to know all about the renegade colt and the unknown kid from Brooklyn who'd come out of nowhere to win the Pennsylvania Gold Cup.

One of the reporters turned to Alec. "Hey, Alec, where's Henry?" he asked. "I don't see him here."

"Oh, he'll be along," Alec said. "I'm sure he's around somewhere."

"Why the change of jocks, Alec?" asked another reporter.

Alec held up his hand. "Hurt my wrist." *They don't need to know any more than that,* he added silently.

Just then, his gaze fell on a man, wearing a familiar-looking fedora, pushing his way through the crowd. The guy looked like a seasoned vet, a bow-legged old-timer with a determined stride. Alec blinked and looked again. It was him, all right. *Henry.*

CHAPTER EIGHTEEN

The Winner's Circle

"There's Henry Dailey now," an attractive blond reporter called, rushing forward to intercept Hopeful Farm's renowned horse trainer. The woman caught Henry by the sleeve. "Terrific win, Henry," she said. "How did Chase coax that kind of ride out of Black Storm?"

"You'll have to ask Creo that," said Henry. "But I can tell you one thing: We are all going to be hearing a lot more about that young man and Black Storm."

Henry was looking straight at Alec now, a curious glint in his icy blue eyes. Even at a distance of fifteen yards, and despite Henry's canned answer, Alec could see the temper seething under the trainer's composed, professional demeanor. *Am I imagining that?* Alec wondered. *Maybe I'm just feeling guilty. Maybe, with a fat check in his pocket, Henry will forget what happened last night.*

Right.

Henry joined Creo, Alec, and a group of reporters beside Storm. In spite of his smile, Alec felt trapped. *Who am I kidding?* he asked himself. Despite the outcome of the race, Henry was never going to forgive Alec for going behind his back. But there had to be some way to put everything in perspective, a way for Alec to make Henry understand why he had done what he did.

The blond reporter was still asking Henry questions. "Is there any truth to the rumor that Storm is shipping to Florida with Luke Stedman?" she asked.

"Ask Alec," Henry answered tersely. "He's the one in charge of Black Storm."

Does Henry really mean that? Alec thought. *Or were those just words for the press?*

The reporter turned to Alec. "How about it, Alec?"

He pulled himself taller.

"No, ma'am," he answered. "Storm is staying at Hopeful Farm for now." He didn't dare look at Henry to see the old trainer's reaction.

"Can we get another picture of all of you together? How about it, Henry? Alec? Creo?"

Alec glanced over at Storm. A few flecks of white foam shone on the rings of his silvery bit. His nostrils flared and his pricked ears were quivering slightly.

"This colt needs to rest," Alec said.

"Come on, Alec," the reporter persisted. "Just a few more questions. It won't take long."

Alec looked at Henry, whose face was expressionless. "Okay. Just a few. But let's hurry it up."

"All right, everybody," a woman said to a group of photographers. "Get in there. That's it."

"Wait a minute," Creo said. He stepped into the crowd and grabbed Mace by the arm. Then he dragged him into the winner's circle. "Come on, Mace. You belong in here, too."

Mace took off his cowboy hat and held it self-consciously to his chest as he took his place with Alec, Henry, Creo, and Storm. The colt looked hot, sweaty, and a little tired. Still, he didn't shy or play, and the photographers managed to get their shots with a minimum of fuss.

The flashbulbs popped, then Alec held up his hands and addressed the crowd. "Okay, everyone. Thank you very much." The fans made way as he led the colt back to the stable area for a well-deserved rest. Storm's job was over, but for Alec, everything was just coming to a head. Henry still hadn't said one word to him.

Back at the tent, Creo and Mace went to get some buckets of hot water, leaving Alec and Henry alone with Storm. The silence that passed between them was painfully awkward.

Alec tried to break the silence. "Well, here we are."

"Yup, you can say that again."

"Yup."

More silence. Finally, Henry cleared his throat.

"Why'd you do it, Alec?" he asked, his voice sounding more disappointed than angry. "How do you think you would feel if I took Black Minx or Satan or another horse and just ran off one day, leaving nothing but a note?"

Alec busied himself straightening Storm's cooler and shooing away a few flies from the colt's ears. "I didn't plan to run off with Storm, Henry. It just sort of happened. It was an impulse."

"Right," Henry grumbled. "An impulse."

Alec stopped fussing over Storm and turned to face the old trainer. "It was the same as when you were going to take a swing at that hijacker the night we got attacked. It was a crazy thing to do, but it seemed right to you at the moment. So you did it."

Henry's eyes flashed, and Alec could tell that he'd struck a delicate nerve.

Storm bobbed his head, and Alec gently clamped his hand across the colt's muzzle. "Easy, Storm," he said.

"Did you see how he ran?" Alec asked Henry softly. "Did you see the race? How *about* this colt?"

"I saw it," Henry said. "So did Stedman. He was plenty mad."

"Yeah?" Alec quickly hid a smile at the thought of having outfoxed Stedman.

"We watched the race together from the rail," Henry said. "After a win like that, he knew there was no way he was going to buy Storm from us for five thousand dollars. So before he left, he pulled ten one-thousand-dollar bills from his wallet and flashed them under my nose."

"Unbelievable. I've never even *seen* a one-thousand-dollar bill."

Henry shook his head. "The guy was carrying ten thousand dollars in his pocket like loose change."

"And?" Alec asked expectantly.

"And what do you think? I told him he'd have to talk with you about that."

Alec's heart pounded. "There aren't any reporters here now, Henry. You don't have to be nice.

It's just you and me. You're really saying Storm can stay?"

Henry gazed at Storm, who was nickering softly. "He earned his keep today. And I suppose Stedman will get over this. He might not be too happy right now, but he's too much of a businessman to let all of this jeopardize his relationship with Hopeful Farm."

Alec hesitated. "What about *our* relationship, Henry?"

"What you did was wrong," Henry said. "But—"

"But what?" Alec asked anxiously.

A slow smile crept over the old trainer's face. "We're family, Alec."

"So you're not mad?"

"Of course I'm mad. I've been mad all day. And I'll be mad for a long, long time."

"I'm sorry, Henry," Alec said sincerely.

Henry shrugged. "Well, I guess things turned out okay. And like you said before, I've been known to make some pretty crazy snap decisions myself." He patted the shirt pocket that held the winning check. "Luckily this one of yours paid off. But next time we're a team—is that a deal?"

Alec put his arm around the old trainer's shoulders. "It's a deal," he said.

About the Author

STEVEN FARLEY is the son of the late Walter Farley, the man who started the tradition with the best-loved horse story of all time, *The Black Stallion*.

A freelance writer based in Manhattan, Steven Farley travels frequently, especially to places where he can enjoy riding, diving, and surfing. Mr. Farley is also the author of *The Black Stallion's Shadow* and co-author of *The Young Black Stallion*.